MIRACULOUS
Miranda

m
i
r
a
c
l
e
s

SIOBHÁN PARKINSON

Hodder
Children's
Books

For the miraculous
Anna O'Mahony

HODDER CHILDREN'S BOOKS

First published in Great Britain in 2016 by Hodder and Stoughton
This paperback edition published in 2017

1 3 5 7 9 10 8 6 4 2

Text copyright © Siobhán Parkinson 2016

The moral right of the author has been asserted.

A CIP catalogue record for this book is available from the British Library.

ISBN 978 1 444 92909 6

Typeset in Fairfield and Garamond by Avon DataSet Ltd,
Bidford-on-Avon, Warwickshire

Printed and bound in Great Britain by Clays Ltd, St Ives plc

The paper and board used in this book are from well-managed forests
and other responsible sources.

Hodder Children's Books
An imprint of Hachette Children's Group
Part of Hodder & Stoughton
Carmelite House,
50 Victoria Embankment,
London, EC4Y 0DZ

An Hachette UK Company
www.hachette.co.uk

www.hachettechildrens.co.uk

They went to sea in a Sieve, they did,
In a Sieve they went to sea;
In spite of all their friends could say,
On a winter's morn, on a stormy day.
In a Sieve they went to sea!
And when the Sieve turned round and round,
And everyone cried, 'You'll all be drowned!'
They called aloud, 'Our Sieve ain't big,
But we don't care a button, we don't care a fig,
In a Sieve we'll go to sea.'
Far and few, far and few,
Are the lands where the Jumblies live;
Their heads are green, and their hands are blue,
And they went to sea in a Sieve.

from 'The Jumblies' by Edward Lear

CHAPTER ONE
The Darren Project

All right, then, I am not going to begin with a whole lot of boring explanations about who I am and what age I am and what my family is like and all that stuff, because I happen to think you can work it out for yourself, as a matter of fact, and if you couldn't be bothered, well then, that's your own business and maybe you would be happier reading a different book.

So in my class we have to learn a new word every day and write down what it means. It is called Word of the Day and the teacher chooses the best one each day and the person who wrote it sticks it up on a special Word Board we have in the classroom, and today I won (I often do, as a matter of fact) and this is what I wrote:

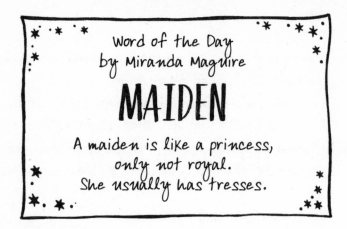

Word of the Day
by Miranda Maguire

MAIDEN

A maiden is like a princess,
only not royal.
She usually has tresses.

If I was allowed to do two Words of the Day, I'd do 'tresses' as well as 'maiden'. Tresses are hair that is long and golden and beautiful. It has nothing to do with trees, which is what Darren Hoey pretends to think it means. Being a boy, Darren thinks he has to make a joke of everything to do with girls. A lot of boys are like that, even the not-so-stupid ones. That is the thing about life.

That is the thing about boys anyway. They make it hard for girls to be nice about them. It must be tough being a boy. They always seem to have to diss girl things, which is stupid because girl things are lovely, as a matter of fact, and boy things are mostly scuffling and tracksuits and horrible haircuts, which are unlovely. I think maybe they are not very happy, boys. I lent Darren my hippo-shaped pencil-rubber once because he'd lost his and he wouldn't use it because it was pink. It wasn't even pink, it was more red that had got a bit old.

'I am going to win Darren Hoey over,' I told Caroline O'Rourke, aka COR, one day after school. COR is my best friend in all the world since we were four years old. 'You mark my words,' I went on. 'I'll have him eating out of—'

'Over what?' she said. 'A barrel?'

Sometimes I wonder what language they speak in COR's house. You can't win someone over a *barrel*.

'Over *to our side*,' I said. 'That's my plan. I'm going to call it the Darren Project.'

'You mean, the girls' side? I don't think Miss Lucey would like that. Boys aren't allowed in the girls' toilets.'

'I never said anything about *toilets*, you dumb-cluck,' I said. 'I mean the side of the angels.'

'We're not angels,' said COR. 'I wouldn't want to be either. Angels are soppy.' She wrinkled her nose.

I sighed. I do love COR. She has a good heart. But she can be hard work, and she is very keen on things not being soppy. I have to watch my step with her.

The reason I call her COR is that those are her initials and COR suits her better than Caroline, in my personal opinion, because that sounds like a queen or something. COR definitely is not queenly. I mean, she wears her hair in bunches. Who ever heard of a queen with bunches?

COR is really good at soccer. I am not really good at soccer. I am really good at Word of the Day. Because of the soccer, COR has to go off after school and pant and get muddy, and I don't, so it is not exactly that football is coming between us, but we are not in the same place at the same time all that often is all. So when we do get a chance to be together, I like to be extra nice to her. I am good at that too. I am super-nice, as a matter of fact.

We are good friends, me and COR, and we bake together on Saturdays. We make apple tarts for the grown-ups and we make chocolate muffins for us. We do not make cupcakes because I will not eat a turquoise thing. Especially not if there are chocolate muffins, which there always are because we make them. (Clever, eh?)

I suppose she is right about angels being soppy, but on the plus side, they get to have tresses. I think tresses would be cool. When I was younger, my hair was blond. Well, OK, it was *fair*. But now it's gone kind of blah-brown (that's what Gemma calls it, she talks that way sometimes), no good at all for tresses. Gemma is my big sister, by the way. I mean, way big. She thinks she knows everything. She does *not* know everything.

'The Darren Project, I am calling it,' I told COR again.

'What are you talking about?'

'This thing about Darren Hoey. I am going to make him do one nice thing for a girl before the end of this term, if it kills me.'

'It probably *will* kill you,' said COR.

I would like a nice funeral, in that case, with singing and flowers. But I didn't say that to COR in case it was too soppy.

CHAPTER TWO
Teeth

Our teacher is mostly nice. When she is cross her voice is like if you dropped something made of iron onto concrete, it hurts your ears. But most of the time she is not doing the iron-on-concrete voice and sometimes she reads us stories, even though we are old enough to read *silently* ourselves. There are often maidens in the stories, with tresses, though she also reads ones for the boys with football in them and fights. COR likes those ones better than the ones with the maidens. I try not to judge.

Her name is Miss Lucey, our teacher. That is not her first name. We do not call teachers by their first name in our school, it's not that kind of school. I know there are schools like that because I have a cousin in Dublin that goes to a school where the teachers have first names. My gran said, 'Get away out of that,' when I told her. That means she doesn't believe you.

Lucey is our teacher's surname, the way other people are called Hoey or O'Rourke. The problem with that is that it means you couldn't be called Lucy for a first name. That is a pity because Lucy is a lovely name. But the thing is, it would be silly to be called the same name twice unless maybe you are a panda. I don't know what Miss Lucey's first name is. I hope it is nice. Amanda or Angelica or something.

Miss Lucey is married. I know that because she went on her honeymoon to Paris last year and she is always banging on about it. I was in Paris once, actually, when I was younger, and I didn't like it much. All pointy little beige stones on the ground and everyone talking French (well, obviously, I suppose). My sister Gemma says stones can't be beige. I said they can – the ones in Paris are beige, so obviously they can. Anyway, the thing about Miss Lucey is that she is still called Miss Lucey, even though she has had a honeymoon and should be called Mrs. I will have to remember to ask her about that.

Only then we had to write an essay for homework and it was not about anything beautiful like tresses but about teeth because we had a lesson about dental hygiene. So this is what I wrote:

Teeth

In my personal opinion, whoever invented teeth didn't do a very good job. Because, look, babies are always roaring their heads off and people say it must be because they are teething. And after all that screaming and roaring and dribbling you only get baby teeth, which are a total waste of time because they fall out anyway, which also hurts, and there is blood.

Toothache is MURDER, and going to the dentist is worse than murder.

When you are old you have to have false teeth, which are gross, although they can be kind of funny too, but that is the only good thing I can think of about teeth.

I think it would be good if teeth were more like fingers, for example. Because you are born with fingers and you don't have to GROW them, and they don't hurt all by themselves, only if you have an accident or something.

When I grow up I will be a scientist like Marie Curie (whose name almost rhymes and nobody even notices) and I will find out a way to cross teeth with fingers.

Marie Curie, almost rhyming scientist

I showed my essay about the teeth to Gemma, because she likes to check my homework (she is dead bossy as a matter of fact), and she said it was all wrong, you are not supposed to write like that for school. You are supposed to research your topic on the internet or in the library and find things out and write them down in your own words and not be saying stupid stuff just out of your head. She always says the things I think up are stupid, which is so not true. I think she gets that idea off the telly, where the older sisters are always rolling their eyes and slamming doors and saying the younger ones are stupid. That is the thing about life.

When I am being Marie Curie, of course I will do my invention properly and people will not end up with a mouthful of fingers or teeth on their hands. Because, in case you haven't been paying attention, I am not stupid.

Gemma said the bit in my essay about Marie Curie

was irrelevant, because Marie Curie wasn't a *geneticist*, which I am glad to hear because that is a horrible word to be. I never said she was, so what is irrelevant about that? *Gemma* is irrelevant, in my personal opinion.

Anyway, I know my teacher will like what I wrote, because it is in my own words and she always likes the things I write because I have a big imagination. That is what she calls it, a big imagination, though I don't really think imaginations are big or small, they don't come in sizes, like shoes or cappuccinos, but I wouldn't argue with her about it because she doesn't like it if you argue. That's the thing about teachers.

That is the difference between school and home. At home it's fine to argue. It is called discussion in our house, and nobody minds, as long as you are not just whining and have proper things to say. I usually do have proper things to say, as a matter of fact.

I would not like you to think Miss Lucey is a mean teacher, though. She is medium cool, actually. For a grown-up.

CHAPTER THREE
Miracles and Riddles

I was right about the Teeth essay. I got a gold star for it. Darren Hoey hissed at me that only babies like getting gold stars, he'd rather get a euro. A euro! He must think teachers are made of money.

That is what my dad is always saying: 'Do you think I am made of money?' It is a lot of nonsense really. It used to scare me a bit when I was younger. I would imagine Dad being made out of all coins and notes and then people coming along and grabbing a fistful of euro-ear or a handful of fingers made out of those rolls of coins you can get from the bank, until there was no Dad left. Just a miserable little pile of one-cent coins that nobody wants and a few scraps of banknotes that people had torn off him.

Anyway, that is all sour grapes with Darren about the

gold star. He'd love to get one, but he can't admit it. Well, yah-boo. I whispered this to COR and she nodded and *then* the teacher said, 'And we have a second gold star today, for an excellent piece of work. Congratulations, Caroline O'Rourke.'

COR went *pink*. She never gets gold stars. She writes very careful essays with the margins all properly ruled and she writes the headings in a different colour. She does it the Gemma way, doing the research and looking up all the hard words in a dictionary. Her essays are very good but quite boring. But that is the thing about life and we are still best friends through thick and thin. I congratulated her on her gold star and she went pink all over again. I've never noticed her blushing before. It made me feel a little bit soppy, actually, the way she was so pleased, and I decided I would try to be more encouraging to her. I am always deciding to try to be nicer to people, but I kind of forget after about fifteen seconds. Though I am basically a super-nice person, of course.

After that we had a poem instead of a story. I wrote the first verse of it at the start of this book so you get the idea. It's quite a long poem but it's really good. I recommend it. COR likes it too and she is not much of a one for poetry, not usually. It is by Edward Lear.

That is his real name, though it sounds like one he made up. I don't know why, but lots of real names sound made up, like Philpot, which is my favourite real name that sounds made up. I might call myself that for a pen-name when I am older. Magillycuddy is a real name too. And Goodenough.

So the people in the poem went to sea in a sieve. I said to the teacher that's mad. You can't do that, you'd drown, because of the holes. It does say that in the poem as a matter of fact, 'You'll all be drowned,' but they go anyway because they don't give a fig. (That is a thing my gran doesn't give either about a lot of things.)

Miss Lucey said it's a miracle. I thought a miracle was like when Jesus raises Lazarus from the dead. I don't think it could be about a sieve that doesn't sink, but the teacher says it's a different kind of miracle.

'What kind?' I asked.

I thought, if we had a miracle in our class it could be about Darren Hoey doing something nice and if I made it happen then I'd be a miracle-worker. I like the sound of that. Like a person in a circus who gets shot out of a cannon or cut in half and glued back together.

'It's when something is impossible,' Miss Lucey said, 'but still you can imagine it.'

Like Darren doing something nice. Impossible, but I

can imagine it – but it would only be a miracle if he actually did it, right? It's not enough for me to imagine it. So it sounds kind of right when Miss Lucey says it, but it's kind of wrong when you think about it. I didn't ask any more, though, because grown-ups get cranky after a while if you keep on asking questions.

Then Miss Lucey said, even without me having to ask, 'Look, Miranda, they bought a monkey with *lollipop paws*.' The people in the poem, she meant, who went to sea in a sieve. (The bit about the monkey with lollipop paws comes later. You have to read more than one verse to get the whole story.)

So? I thought, but I didn't say it out loud, because there is a rule against it in our school. It is a stupid rule, but a lot of rules in school are stupid. You would be worn out with them.

Lollipop paws are a great idea for a monkey. I made a drawing of that, only you wouldn't know the monkey was a monkey. He looks a bit like Darren Hoey, as a matter of fact. I showed it to Miss Lucey but she didn't notice the resemblance. Just as well.

I think what Miss Lucey really means by a miracle is when somebody writes something that is kind of amazing only it is out of their imagination, like the poem about the lollipop paws and the sieve, and this is different from when you write about teeth and it is all dentition and enamel and molars. I bet COR used those words in her Teeth essay, but personally I would never make any of them a Word of the Day.

There is a different kind of miracle that people talk about on the telly in Gran's house and that is a Miracle of Modern Medicine. Miracles of Modern Medicine are things like keyhole surgery and amazing drugs. The drugs are usually a cure for cancer, because that is the most popular disease. Like, there was this boy who lived about a mile away from us and he had to have some miracle treatment that they only do in a special hospital in America and there was this big campaign and everyone did cake sales and pub quizzes and parachute jumps and they collected loads of money to send him and his mum to America. I'd rather go to Eurodisney, but they'd never do parachute jumps for *that*. I think it did work for a while, but everyone was going around whispering about him and staring at his sisters in school and saying how *sad* it all was.

Anyway, he was good for a while after he came back from America so it must have been a little bit miraculous but then he got sick again and so they had more pub quizzes and cake sales and this time they sent him to Lourdes.

I saw a programme about Lourdes once. You get a different kind of miracle there. Mostly it is very sick people who go to Lourdes in their wheelchairs or whatever and they have to pray and then sometimes they are cured and that is the miracle. But mostly it doesn't work. That is what Gemma says. She also says that if anyone ever gets any ideas about doing a pub quiz for *her*, she will personally strangle them, which is a thing I would like to see, as a matter of fact. That is because she is very private, Mum says.

I asked Gemma what about Eurodisney and she said, '*What* about Eurodisney?'

She is starting to talk in riddles, in my personal opinion. She is almost sixteen, which makes her nearly an adult. I have noticed that adults talk in riddles a lot. And the older they get, the worse they get. That is why nobody knows what the blazes Gran is saying. (Except when she says 'what the blazes' I do know that 'blazes' is instead of 'hell', because in Gran's opinion you are not supposed to say the H-word, which just shows you how much Gran is for the birds.) But Gemma used not to talk in riddles, so I am a bit sad about that. Soon I will be the only normal person in the house who says what they mean.

He died in the end, the boy that went to America, so

the miracle treatment wasn't all that good, although Gran says people often get better from cancer (which is true, I know) and I am not to be going on about people dying, it is too upsetting. But the thing is, he might as well have gone to Eurodisney after all. It was very sad. I cried about it, even though I didn't really know him.

We don't talk about Gemma's 'condition' much in our family, as a matter of fact. She says it is bad enough being a patient when she is in the hospital but that she is not going to put up with it when she is at home as well, so it's a kind of forbidden topic in our house. Outside the house too, of course. Nobody in my school has a clue, for example. You get used to it. I mean, you get used to her being sick, but you also get used to not talking about it, and sometimes you sort of just forget about it. Only not really.

They never tell us about Lourdes in RE. RE is all about being kind to each other, which we know anyway. At least, I know it and COR knows it, though not Darren Hoey I suppose. I'd rather it was more about angels and apparitions, that would be much more interesting. I'd love to see an apparition.

That's the thing about school. They only teach you what they think you should know instead of asking what you would like to know. When I am older I will probably invent a different kind of school. I might ask Miss Lucey to help me with it if she is not dead yet.

I do kind of think it would be great if there really were miracles.

CHAPTER FOUR
Fantasy Geography

I was explaining Fantasy Geography to COR at school yesterday, when Darren Hoey came lolloping by, grinning stupidly at us and asking us what we were gossiping about. We don't gossip. We are not that kind of girl, either of us.

Actually, I got the idea for Fantasy Geography from Darren, in a way, because he plays a game called Fantasy Football. That sounds nicer than it actually is. It's when you make up football teams and they play your friends' made-up teams. I think. I don't know how the made-up teams score any goals. Maybe you can make up scores too, but then everyone would make up ridiculous scores because they would all want to win, so that can't be right. It is a mystery. That is what my gran says when she doesn't know the answer to something. You are supposed to think that is an amazing thing, but after a while you get to know it is just her way of not admitting that she hasn't a clue about anything.

You'd like my gran, only she talks Gran Speak (that is what Gemma calls it), which is hard to learn. Some of it is actually Latin, like her cat is called Tantum Ergo, except she doesn't tell the vet that in case he would be shocked. I asked her what Tantum Ergo meant, and she said it is Latin for 'so much therefore', which in my personal opinion is weird but not very shocking.

Dad told me that it is only shocking because it is a hymn.

I said, 'Why is it shocking that it is a hymn?'

And he said, 'Do you not think it is a bit shocking to call a cat by the name of a hymn?'

'Not really,' I said. 'But I suppose Latin and English are all the same to a cat anyway.'

Gran lives with us a lot of the time. Her real house is about three miles away and sometimes she cycles home to get stuff, or to feed Tantum if he is sulking too much to have his dinner at our house, or to just get a bit of peace. That is what she says. A bit of peace. That is meant to be a dig at us. Honestly, you would think we were always shouting and screaming at each other, the way Gran goes on about needing peace, and we are not a bit like that. The opposite, as a matter of fact. We are all very polite in my house, even when we are having an argument. I mean, a discussion. Not like in COR's house, where they really are always shouting and screaming and banging doors and the bathroom is flooded half the time and the dog sleeps on the parents' bed and on Saturdays everyone cooks their own dinner so there is a lot of clattering of saucepans and squabbling over the peppermill. It is quite exciting. I like going over there for a bit of noise, actually.

Anyway, Darren's Fantasy Football thing gave me the idea for Fantasy Geography and I was just saying to COR that I think I will patent it.

'What does that mean?' she asked. She is always asking me what words mean, because I am the word expert. I like that in a friend, shows loyalty.

'That is what you do with inventions,' I explained. 'So people can't steal them.'

Fantasy Geography is much more fun than real geography, because for that you have to learn a whole lot of things like population and capital cities and trade winds, none of which is at all interesting, but for Fantasy Geography, you just make places up.

'What is the *point*?' Darren Hoey butted in.

COR rolled her eyes. She has no time for Darren. Even less than me.

'How do you mean, the point?' I said. 'It's just for fun, like, it's a *game*. Games don't have points.'

COR gave a smirk and tossed her bunches to show she agreed with me.

'Yes they do,' Darren said. 'How do you *win*?'

That is such a *boy* question.

'You don't,' I told him. 'You just make places up, and the more you imagine your place, the more interesting it gets. You can keep adding things like rivers and animals and cities with amazing names and astonishing mountain ranges made of . . .' I hesitated. I hadn't decided what they were made of.

'Rock,' said COR decisively.

'*All* mountain ranges are made of rock,' Darren said, narrowing his eyes.

Darren's eyes are pretty narrow to begin with, as a matter of fact, so when he narrows them they kind of disappear.

'The *edible* sort,' I said with a sigh that was supposed to mean *Really, Darren, get a grip*, and COR gave a little giggly snort.

But Darren is slow on the uptake. He just sneered

and said, 'Oooh, *edible*. Is that your Word of the Day, Miss Miranda-pants?'

That name is supposed to make me feel bad. But it isn't even properly rude. I wouldn't say I exactly *like* being called not-very-rude names, but it doesn't really bother me. Darren probably does it because he never wins Word of the Day and he is just jealous.

Toblerone would be better for mountain ranges, I thought afterwards, but I didn't say that to Darren, because he had already snarled and run off, and I don't see why I should tell him my best ideas when he is so horrible. At this rate, I am never going to be able to make him do something nice and the Darren Project will end in failure. COR has said this all along. She can't imagine Darren ever doing anything even remotely friendly.

I made a drawing of my fantasy country, which is called Magnanimous, only it is more like a map with labels on things so you know what they are called and what they are for. I have decided it is an island, because all the best countries are, in my personal opinion, especially Ireland and Iceland. I have never been to Iceland but a place that has geysers has to be good (my gran does not agree about that, but that's Gran for you).

I made a city too, called Splendiferous, with silver

gates around it and giraffes for police, because they can see over the roofs and catch the burglars in their mouths and give them a good shaking and all the swag comes rattling out of their pockets and backpacks, diamonds and goldy things and cutlery with curlicues on the handles. 'Curlicues' is a Gran word, but I like it, not like most of her words. Also, they get dizzy and headachy, the burglars, and their bones hurt from being shaken, which is better than going to jail for making people stop being burglars and also much cheaper.

I think it is a miracle kind of place, actually.

I wanted to tell Gemma all this when I came home from school, about the Fantasy Geography and Darren calling me names and COR having a giggle about him, but I could see she wasn't listening. When she gets a coughing fit, she really can't concentrate on anything except coughing. It is very annoying, it hurts your ears. Sometimes you could wish that if a person in your family is going to have an illness it could be a nice quiet dignified kind of a one, like her legs not working or something, like Katy (in *What Katy Did*).

Actually, I don't really wish that, because (a) there is no point and (b) there is probably no calm and dignified kind of illness anyway; there usually is spit and sweat and grunting, no matter what is wrong with a person and (c) it is much worse for them than it is for you, so you should not even be wishing like that. Anyway, you do get sort of used to the coughing, except I don't like it when it goes on in the night, because you think she is going to choke or swallow her tongue or something.

Darren Hoey told me once about this man that swallowed his tongue, which is a gross idea and I don't believe it, because your tongue is anchored in your mouth, it couldn't like, *unhook*, and go down your swallow. I know that, but in the middle of the night, things like that seem very real.

I *hate* Darren Hoey.

CHAPTER FIVE
The Tooth Fairy Messes Up

COR has a theory that the Tooth Fairy stops coming when you are about eight. I don't think that's fair. I think it should go on as long as you still have teeth falling out.

'But you can still be losing teeth when you are, like, *twelve*,' she said. 'You could be in *secondary* school.'

I don't see what that has to do with anything. Teeth are teeth, and if the Tooth Fairy wants them, she should jolly well come and get them and who cares what age you are?

The reason we were having this conversation is that I lost a back tooth yesterday. It came out when I was eating peanuts. At first I thought it *was* a peanut, because it didn't hurt or bleed the way the front ones did. So even though I am quite old for losing teeth, I put my tooth in a glass of water by my bed like always and hoped for the best.

My mum came into my room this morning in the middle of the night. I mean, technically it was morning but it was pitch-black out. I thought she was checking up on the Tooth Fairy, but she said Gemma had got worse and they were taking her to the hospital and I was to be good for Gran.

It would be more like it if they told Gran to be good for me. But that would never occur to them. Grown-ups always gang up to tell the kids to be good, even if the problem person is one of the grown-ups and not a kid. Not that Gran is exactly a problem, but she is definitely daft as a brush.

I don't panic about Gemma going to hospital any more. I used to bawl my head off when I was younger. I didn't know what a hospital was. I thought it must be like going to prison or something because when Gemma had to go there, everyone got very sad and prickly and silent and they wouldn't tell me what was going on and I didn't know if she was ever going to be allowed to come home. I thought it must be that Gemma had done something terrible and shameful and we all had to pretend it hadn't happened. It made me feel really horrible. All choked up and terrified. So then I would stage a tantrum because I didn't know what else to do to make people talk to me. That would drive my mother mad and she would nearly have a tantrum herself, actually, she would be so angry with me, but, hey, I was only small.

I don't do that any more, of course, because I know what hospital is about now. But still, when she has to go in suddenly like that, I can feel myself getting a bit edgy and I have these unreasonable thoughts like, *Could she not have waited until breakfast time?* But I don't say it out loud. It wouldn't be right. But still, I am allowed at least to *think* that. In my personal opinion.

It is very hard to get back to sleep when someone wakes you up in the middle of the night, so I got up and sat at my desk for a while and I took out my map of Magnanimous and I did a bit more inventing so I wouldn't have to think about Gemma being sick and Mum and Dad being worried and me being stuck with Gran, because those are not good thoughts and inventing Fantasy Geography stuff *is* a good thought.

The Tooth Fairy didn't leave any money either. I am not best pleased. That is the thing about life. As soon as one thing goes wrong, something else happens to make you feel even worse.

I wish they had let me see Gemma before she left. I

would have told her it was all right that she gets so cross with me and that I forgave her. That is the kind of thing people do on the telly when other people are sick. They tell them how much they love them and all, though I don't think I would actually go that far, because I am practising not being soppy and it is not like she is going to die or anything.

As far as I know.

I never thought about that before. But I suppose . . .

That thought makes me feel dizzy. I won't think it.

I am not usually allowed to go and see her when she is in hospital because of being a child. I think that is appalling discrimination. Mum says I should send her texts, but you can't say much in a text really, can you?

My life is not all that very great right now as a matter of fact. It is lucky I have Fantasy Geography to cheer me up.

CHAPTER SIX
Gran's Terrible Secret

I have made an amazing discovery. It is *truly* astonishing.
It is more amazing even than Fantasy Geography.

Gran . . . is

a . . .
Secret ...
Smoker!!!!!!!!!!

Only now they are all away, it is not a secret, she
does it in FRONT of me, as if I was Tantum Ergo
and couldn't tell on her. Which of course I won't do,
but I'd rather she didn't take it for granted. She goes
around with her cigarette actually *in her mouth*, and she
talks around it, and there is ash hanging off the end of
it. I keep expecting it to fall on my hair and set me on
fire or something. But the thing is, I am pretending
I don't notice, because that seems to be the way I am

supposed to behave, so I can't say, 'Please be careful with that ash on the end of your cigarette, Gran,' because I am not supposed to have noticed that there even *is* a cigarette.

I wish they would come home, my parents, or they might never see their younger daughter again. I could be a little heap of ashes with just my shoes on top, like Harriet who played with matches and was burnt 'with all her clothes and arms and hands and eyes and nose', all except 'her little scarlet shoes'. Only it would all be Gran's fault, not mine. They'd be sorry if I was a heap of ashes with only my shoes left. *Here lies Miranda Maguire, a martyr to the smokes.*

The story of Harriet who got burnt to death is from another poem we did at school, by the way. Miss Lucey is great at finding poems that have good stories in them. It is supposed to be about not playing with matches, but it is mostly for the laugh, in my personal opinion.

Which reminds me, I asked Miss Lucey why she isn't Mrs now and she said because there is no Mr Lucey. So then I asked her how come she didn't have to change her name when she got married and she said you don't have to if you don't want to. Which I didn't know before, because my mum and dad have the same name. I think that is fairer and I will not change my name if I get married, because I like being called Maguire. It is nice to hear about things you didn't know before, especially when it's useful information like this.

I wish I had scarlet shoes, like Harriet. But mostly I wish I had a normal family. I told COR that – about the shoes, not about the family – because she doesn't know anything about my family being all stressed out and Gemma being sick and being in hospital and Gran practically trying to commit suicide with cigarettes. She said she would rather have football boots. Everyone is different, I suppose.

It's worse it's getting. That is one of Gran's favourite sentences, and I never thought I would hear myself using it, but there is no other way to say this. Gran has started using her *hand* as an ashtray. When her cigarette ash gets to the point where I am going to explode with the tension about where it is going to fall, she suddenly cups her left hand, takes her cig out of her mouth with her right hand, and taps the ash into the cup of her left hand. And then she walks around a bit more, before she finally realises that she can't go around all day with her left hand cupped in front of her and she goes off and empties it into a bin.

It is wearing me out.

Then I had a great idea. We had to write another one

of those essays like the teeth one, only this one was about 'any health-related issue', so I wrote this.

Lung Cancer

This is what you get if you smoke. The more you smoke, the more likely you are to get it. It does not matter how expert a smoker you are. Even if you can walk around with a cigarette in your mouth and talk at the same time, you can still get lung cancer from it.

It is not a nice way to die. There are probably not many nice ways to die, but if there were, lung cancer would not be one of them.

Marie Curie, the Rhyming Scientist, invented a cure for cancer. Or not exactly, because it actually GAVE her cancer, which is extremely sad, but that meant she was a kind of martyr. That is all very well if you are a rhyming scientist but it is not so good if you are in my family and I would like you to be around for a while yet.

You can also get a lot of other diseases from smoking, so if you are lucky enough not to get lung cancer, one of the other ones is sure to get you. (I am not even counting the possibility of setting your apron string on fire, like Harriet.) I know those other diseases you can get from smoking are not relevant to this essay, because it is supposed to be about lung cancer and not about not-lung-cancer, but it is relevant to people who smoke.

What makes it so awful is that there are people who are sick and it is not their fault AT ALL. And then along come these other people with perfectly good lungs and they just muck them up with disgusting sticky tar and stuff. That is such a waste of perfectly good lungs. It makes me very angry.

Gran asked me what kind of tommyrot I was writing now. I don't exactly know what tommyrot is, but you can probably get it from smoking. You can get most things from smoking, as a matter of fact. So I showed her what I had written, because that was the whole point of writing it, obviously. I kind of expected that she would pale and say, 'Oh, you poor darling,' and clasp me to her tear-stained, bony bosom and promise she would give up smoking forthwith, but she didn't do that. (Actually, I must write a Word of the Day about 'forthwith', which means immediately, only funnier.)

What Gran actually said was, '"God bless us and save

us," said old Mrs Davis, "I never knew herrin's were fish",' which is a rhyme she always says when she doesn't know what to say and thinks it is best to make a joke of things. It is not much of a joke either. It makes you go heh-heh, but it is not the chortle-chortle kind of super-funny that Gran thinks it is: it doesn't make you burst out laughing.

But then instead of laughing Gran burst into tears and ran out of the room. That was a bit of an over-reaction, in my personal opinion. I mean, I wasn't wishing that she would get lung cancer or anything. The opposite, actually.

I was alarmed at that, as a matter of fact. I thought I might have given her a stroke or something, which is another thing that smokers get, but she came back after a while and she muttered something I didn't understand and then she made the tea, so it was all's well that ends well.

I added one more bit to my essay before I went to bed and it was this:

I have told my gran that and she agrees with me but it is probably too late. She has already succumbed.

I didn't want to end with being angry, as that sounded a bit heavy. And I like 'succumbed'. It means that Gran has given in and let the cigarettes take her over.

I got a star for that essay as well, as a matter of fact, and the teacher asked me if it would be all right if she read it out to the whole class. She doesn't usually do that. She thinks it is embarrassing for the person who wrote it if everyone has to listen to what they wrote, but I didn't mind. I suppose she must have wanted people to learn a good lesson about smoking and its dreadful consequences.

When she had finished reading it, there were tears in Miss Lucey's eyes, and she said to the class, 'I think Miranda deserves a round of applause, don't you?' which I thought was a bit much, actually. It is only giving out about smoking really, I don't see why everyone had to make such a big deal of it, but that's teachers for you, you never know how they are going to react.

Darren Hoey came up to me in break and said, 'I'm sorry about your gran.'

I stared at him. It sounded as if he was trying to be nice, which was weird in itself, but apart from that, it was very puzzling. There isn't anything the matter with my gran.

COR said, 'Oh buzz off, Darren Hoey, and mind your

own business,' which I didn't understand either. She put her hand on my shoulder and gave it a little pat, as if something terrible had happened.

The thing is, something kind of terrible *has* happened, what with Gemma being poorly and going to hospital and all, but nobody knows about that. All they know about is that smoking is bad for you, which is what I wrote.

'What's wrong with everyone today?' I asked, and COR gave me a very strange look, and I said '*What?*' And she said, 'Oh, nothing,' but I knew that meant *Oh, something*. Weird.

Anyway, listen, there has been a kind of a minor miracle. Gran has given up smoking. Or at least she has stopped doing it when I am in the room, which is all I can say for sure. That would not be as good as stopping altogether, but better than nothing, in my personal opinion, because at least I am not going to be a victim of passive smoking. And it could be that she has given it up altogether, for all I know.

It is not as good a miracle as it would be if you grew teeth on your hands, but it is pretty good, and the best part is that it is because of something I wrote.

I could get good at this. Miranda the Miracle Maker. Has a ring to it, don't you think?

CHAPTER SEVEN
Texting

My dad came home yesterday evening to get some extra PJs and things for Gemma, and her iPhone, which she obviously didn't think of taking with her in the middle of the night. (I don't know how come she gets to have an iPhone. Maybe it is because she is older or maybe it is because she is sick. I would love an iPhone, but I can't be jealous if it is because she is sick. That is the thing about my life. It is not just that it is not fair but you aren't allowed even to *think* that it is not fair.) So that means Gemma is going to be in the hospital for a long stint, because obviously you don't need all your stuff if you are only staying for a night or two. Which is a bit worrying if it is your sister.

It is always horrible when Gemma has to go to hospital. Mum goes all weepy and Dad starts trying to be strong, which doesn't suit him, and I get landed with Gran. Don't get me wrong, I love Gran, but she is like orange squash. You need to take her in small doses and *dilute* her. So I always imagined it must be horrible for Gemma too, being away from home, not having her stuff around her, not being able to join in the family chit-chat, all that. As well as being sick and all, of course.

But she told me before that once they get her medication right and she starts not to feel so sick, it's kind of fun being in hospital. There's a whole gang of them that have been friends since they were small, and they meet each other in hospital quite often. Sometimes she meets Jennifer, who is her best hospital friend, and everyone pretends to think they are twins because they are the same age and height and hair colour and they call them Jen and Gem. If one of them is in hospital, the other one goes to see her, but often they are in at the same time, and they are real close, closer than COR and me, if I am honest, and I can't help feeling they are lucky like that. And then there are other friends too that you hear about. There's Josh and Sarah and Ciara and Eamon and Freda.

Dad asked me if there was anything I would like to send to Gemma. I think he meant love and kisses or something or maybe a card, but I thought it might be nice to send her an actual thing to cheer her up. The first thing I thought of was Lucy Fur, who is my teddy. She is not named after my teacher. I had Lucy Fur long before I ever even heard of Miss Lucey. It is just a coincidence that their names sound the same.

You might think that I am too old to have a teddy. That is where you would be wrong. She talks.

If I were in hospital, my talking bear is definitely what I would want, but I would miss her terribly and I am not all that sure that Gemma would really appreciate her. Lucy never talks to her anyway. So instead I gave Dad *Treasure Island* for Gemma to read. I have tried reading it, but I am not ready for it yet. I may never be. I think maybe you have to be a boy. It is the kind of book they give you for Christmas because they read it when they were young. Gemma is not a boy, obviously, but she fancies herself as a great reader, so we'll see how she gets on with it. She can tell me the story when she gets home and then I can decide if it is worth reading. (Good plan, eh?)

So anyway Gemma sent me a text today. She doesn't text me much. Well, I mean, we live in the same house. We can do the talking thing. But even when she is away, she doesn't text much. Mum says it's because she doesn't know what to say to me. There's always *Hello, sis, how are you? XXX*. That'd do fine. But no, she doesn't seem to think that's worth texting. I don't text her either, I suppose, but I'm the baby sister. I can't be the one to go writing *Hello, sis*, etc. That's not the way things work.

To be fair, she only got her phone last night.

Anyway, the text she sent today was to say that Curly Wurly sends his best to me. (I never really understand that phrase. His best *what?*)

Curly Wurly is a nickname for Josh, who is one of Gemma's hospital friends. It is not his real nickname, it is just me that calls him that. I have met him a few times and think he is cute. I also think he and Gemma are a bit more than friends. He is the same age as her, but taller. I call him Curly Wurly partly because he has lovely coppery curls.

The other reason I call him Curly Wurly is that one day Gemma had to go off for some test or, I don't know, physio or something, and it was her turn at Scrabble so I made a word instead of her and it was 'zealous'. I did not know what it meant but I knew how to spell it because I read it in a book once. It was seven letters on a triple letter score and I won about fifty-five million points for it and Josh said he would give me a Curly Wurly if I did not let on I had made that word for Gemma. But I would not because I do not much like Curly Wurlys, I am more a Crunchie kind of person, and he was fuming and I was laughing my head off when Gemma came back. She said she could not take that score because she had not made the word herself. That calmed him down and in the end Gemma won anyway. So that's nice. That he's there, I mean.

She also told me in the text they have new curtains on her ward. With roses on them. Fascinating. You have to be there, I suppose.

And they are making her eat more. She is always progging her face, as a matter of fact. She is supposed to eat extra calories. It is good for her, it seems, which is, well, kind of *useful*, I have to say. Not that I don't believe her, it's just that, well, it'd be nice if someone said to me one day, 'Hey, Miranda, would *you* like a second cheeseburger?' Just now and again. If, you know, there were extra cheeseburgers knocking about.

So apparently it's ice cream at the moment, because she can't face all the other stuff. I'm not all that gone on ice cream myself, as a matter of fact. It hurts my nose.

She said to tell Gran that Alva is pregnant and she put in a whole lot of exclamation marks and smiley faces and also an immensely cross face, thunderous, actually. I don't know who Alva is, but I told Gran anyway, and she blew a fuse. (That must be what the thunderous face was about.) Apparently, Alva is not married and that drives Gran bananas. She thinks you should always be married first and then get pregnant. I don't know why. Maybe it's a bit like putting the milk in your tea first instead of the other way around. Some people get very hot and bothered about that. You couldn't be up to people really, they wear me out.

She forgot to say thank you for *Treasure Island*. Or maybe Dad forgot to give it to her. Or maybe she hates it and thinks it is more tactful to say nothing? It's hard to work out what people think when you are looking right at them, but it's impossible when all you have is a text message. But I texted her back anyway.

Gran is well. So am I.
We miss you. And Mum and Dad.
Is the tooth fairy a fake?
M

I was dying to send my love to Curly Wurly, but in the end I didn't say anything about him. I didn't want her thinking I was *muscling in* or anything. But he is dead cute. He really is.

Gemma didn't reply for ages, but just before I went to sleep my phone beeped, and there was a text from her:

Mum says the tooth fairy is
a wuss and is very sorry.
xxx

I don't know what Mum has to do with it. You couldn't be up to people, in my personal opinion.

CHAPTER EIGHT
A Blackbird and a Saxophone

There was a singing test today at school. Nobody told us why. I am quite good at singing, though not as good as I am at Fantasy Geography and Word of the Day. But – wait till you hear this – *Darren Hoey* has this fabulous voice. He's a proper little blackbird, Miss Lucey said.

I think he was kind of embarrassed and kind of proud at the same time. I am glad he was embarrassed, because if he was only proud he would be murder to be around. I mean, he is murder to be around anyway, so I suppose I mean he would be *mass* murder to be around. But it is good that he can sing because I was beginning to think there was no point at all to him, and now it seems that there is something he can do after all. It gives me hope for the Darren Project, which I had almost forgotten about.

'See? If you wait long enough,' I said to COR, 'you will probably find that everyone has a point.'

'What are you talking about, Miranda A. Maguire?' She always uses my full name when she thinks I am being silly. I don't know how she knows about the A part. *Nobody* knows about that.

'Darren,' I said. 'He can sing.'

'Your point being?'

She can be sarky, COR.

'Well, he's good for something.'

COR looked as if she was going to argue, so I took out my map of Magnanimous and showed her the glass hospital I'd put on it.

'Why is there a hospital?' COR asked suspiciously.

'To make the children better.'

'Oh!' she said. 'A hospital for sick *children*.'

'Only I call it the Glass Hospital for Getting-better Children.'

'Why?' asked COR.

'Because it's stupid to call it a hospital for sick children. *Well* children don't need a hospital.'

'Your point being?' she said again.

I don't know where she picked up that phrase, it's most annoying. I didn't bother to explain that since hospitals are, by definition, for sick people, then it is just a waste to put the word 'sick' in the name of one. Also, 'getting better' is much more cheerful.

'And why is it on the side of a mountain?' she asked then, peering at the map.

It was just a question, but it felt like an attack.

'I didn't want it to be in the city with all noise and buses,' I said. 'And the reason it is glass is so the sick children can all see out and watch the birds flying and the mountain goats hopping from rock to rock and hear their little bells tinkling. Like in *Heidi*, you know?'

She gave the faintest bit of a nod. I took that as a good sign and I went on to explain about how the patients in this hospital all have hammocks instead of beds, because that is more fun, and the medicines taste like jelly beans. The doctors go about with liquorice twists around their necks so you know they are doctors and not just porters or lab workers in white coats. And the children are allowed to have their pets in the ward, as long as they are glass-house-trained and speak Pianissimo or, at a push, Diminuendo.

'Whoa, there a minute!' COR said. '*What* did you say they have to speak?'

'Oh, yeah,' I said. 'I forgot to explain before about the languages in Magnanimous. The people there speak Music. Different kinds of people speak different kinds of Music, like the granddads speak Adagio and the toddlers speak Allegretto and the dogs speak Pianissimo, which is a very good language for dogs, because it means extremely quietly and dogs do mostly need to pipe down, right?'

'You mean, those Italian words they write on music to tell you how to play it?' she said. (She learns piano. As well as playing football. She is very busy. I don't seem to have time for things like that.) 'Those are the languages that people speak in this mad place of yours with the glass hospital?'

'Yes,' I said.

'Why?' she said.

'No why,' I said. 'Just because.'

My dad taught me those words. He is mad into music. He told me that all the words in music are Italian. When I am older I will learn Italian, because I like the sound of it. At the moment, I only know *Mi chiamo Miranda* (My name is Miranda) and *Un gelato per favore* (An ice cream please), which is what Dad calls 'Survival Italian'.

Except I don't need to survive in Italy because I have never been there, but you never know your luck. That's what Dad says. I bet I would like it better than Paris.

But I am not a big fan of ice cream, as I've said, so really it is very stupid that that is the only thing I know how to order in Italian. That is the thing about life. You often learn the wrong stuff.

I said that to COR and she said she likes ice cream so I could give it to her. She is a *ridiculous* girl.

But even so, I told her some more about the Glass Hospital, about how the nurses read bedtime stories, but of course, because most of the patients are in bed all the time, it is *always* story time, so it is a very happy place and nobody is ever lonely or sad or frightened. There are also trees inside, to make the air clean, and parrots live in the trees and brighten the place up a treat. The needles for the injections and the drips and everything are made of ice, and they are very sharp but you don't feel them going in because they are so cold and they just melt away before you feel them. It is the same with the knives for the operations.

COR laughed a few times and smiled a lot, so I think she must have liked it. She never laughs just to be polite.

I did not win Word of the Day today because Darren

won with 'tommyrot', which is an ace word, but he totally stole it from me. He must have heard me telling COR about Gran saying it.

I forgive him, though, because I have a kind nature, and it is only right that poor old Darren gets to win sometimes, even if he has to cheat. I told COR that and she said she was sorry.

'But it was Darren, not you,' I said.

'I know,' she said. 'But I'm sorry anyway. I'm sorry that Darren stole your word.'

She gave me this big Bambi-eyed look and she put her hand on my arm and said it again. If it hadn't been Caroline O'Rourke, I'd have thought she was being soppy.

'Oh, Miranda, I'm so sorry. Especially considering . . .'

'What?' I said. 'Considering what, exactly?'

'What you're *going through*,' she whispered, and I swear there was this weird shininess on her eyeballs as if – well, almost as if there were unshed tears in her eyes.

'What are you talking about, you daft girl?' I said, but she just blinked and gave my arm another little squeeze.

It is very puzzling. She doesn't even know that Gemma is sick, never mind in hospital. I *told* you she was ridiculous.

When the singing tests were over, they explained what it was all about. Apparently there is going to be a concert in the town hall and they want children for it and that is us. Darren is going to be Oliver Twist and me and COR and most of the rest of the class are going to be the Other Orphans and we have to sing *Consider yourself – At home* and a few more songs.

I was telling Gran all about this when I got home today and she keeps thinking it is Annie, but that is a totally different orphan in a totally different musical, which she says is very confusing (which it isn't), and then she starts on about 'Annie Get Your Gun', who isn't an orphan at all, so I don't see the connection. She is a trial, Gran, which is Miss Lucey's word for people who drive you up the wall.

Miss Lucey told us that all the Other Orphans are supposed to be boys (I can't imagine why), so we have to wear caps on backwards and paint streaks on our faces with burnt corks. I can understand about the streaks, but I don't understand how a cap that is backwards is supposed to make you look more like a boy. COR says it is about scooping our hair up but I don't see why you have to do that backwards. If you are going to scoop, you might as well do it forwards, but there you go, where there are adults there are very weird ideas and if you want to be a happy child the best thing is to get used to it.

I suppose there must come a time, maybe when you turn eighteen and get the vote, when it All Becomes Clear. I can't wait. Though obviously it all gets a bit blurry again when you get old, if Gran is anything to go by.

Lucy Fur liked the Glass Hospital when I told her about it and all the languages. But she wanted to know how the people in Magnanimous understand each other if they all speak different languages, like Opera and Allegro and Drumroll.

So I made up the Saxophone of Modulation. This is a special Magnanimous translating machine. You hold it while you are speaking and the Saxophone of Modulation translates it into other kinds of Music and out it comes in notes that other people can understand. Lucy Fur said that was brilliant, which in my personal opinion is probably correct. She and I often see eye to eye about things, as a matter of fact. I am glad I didn't send her up to the hospital in Dublin to Gemma instead of *Treasure Island*. I hope that is not selfish of me.

CHAPTER NINE
Up in Nellie's Room

Miss Lucey was banging on all the time about Darren being such a blackbird with his *mellifluous* voice. So I said, how do you spell that, because I'd never heard that word before, so she spelt it out and then she broke it up for me like this:

MELL (as in *pell-mell*)
I (as in *in*, not as in *I*)
FLU (as in *fluid*)
OUS (as in *curious* or *humorous*)

I thought that was a savage word, so I wrote it down and I looked it up and the next day I did it for Word of the Day:

Word of the Day
MELLIFLUOUS
By Miranda Maguire
Flowing and sweet-sounding,
as if honey had a voice

I *so* won with *that*! Darren Hoey can stuff his 'tommyrot'.

If by any chance Darren managed to sneak into Magnanimous, he would not speak Mellifluous, even if he is 'a proper little blackbird' in real life. I have made up a language for him, in case of a Darren emergency, and it is called Diaboloso. I had to get Dad to help me with that one.

Gran reads to me when I am in bed, and it is very cosy and she is not so annoying as during the daytime, and then sometimes we talk afterwards and she tells me all about The Olden Days, when she was young and there was no electricity and you had to boil the water on the range. At least, that is what I used to think, but she laughed at me when I said that and said she was only *my* gran, not *her* gran, who did boil water on the range, as a matter of fact, but that really *was* The Olden Days.

When Gran was young there *was* electricity but the

television was black and white and they didn't invent colour television until the snooker got popular and people complained they couldn't follow it in black and white. Which just goes to show that there is a reason for snooker, even though it looks like the most pointless activity on the face of the earth. It is astonishing, in my personal opinion, how there is more to so many things than you might think, like Darren for example, turning out to have a point after all (even if he did steal my word on me). That is a cheerful thought. I like to have cheerful thoughts whenever I can.

When I got home today, Gran was pacing up and down, muttering to herself. She had her glasses up on top of her head like a hairband and a row of yellow stickies flapping on the sleeve of her cardigan. She is always sticking little notes to her clothes so she won't forget things.

She said, 'Your father rang. Do you want the good news or the bad news?' as if we were on some TV comedy programme, but she wasn't laughing.

'The bad news,' I said. I always believe in getting bad stuff over with.

She pulled a sticky off her sleeve and read, 'Gemma v. sick.'

Well, we kind of knew that. People don't go to hospital for the *craic*.

I shrugged. 'And the good news?'

'New miracle drug,' Gran read off the next sticky.

'Oh?' I perked up. That *was* good. Until I remembered about that boy that went to America.

Gran put up her hand and said, 'Wait, there's a bit of bad news that goes with that. It costs a million pounds, the miracle drug.'

My heart sank. All the glow of winning Word of the Day with 'mellifluous' was draining away.

'Euro,' I said automatically. Gran's always forgetting, even though there have been euro instead of pounds since before I was even born.

'Euro,' she agreed.

'Where would we get a million euro, Gran?' I asked.

And Gran said, 'Up in Nellie's room behind the wallpaper.' Which is a typical Gran thing to say. It means absolutely nothing and it sounds weird and you are not supposed to question it.

Gran plucked another note off her sleeve and squinted at it. 'Your dad said to tell you that Gemma sends her love,' she added. 'And there is also love from someone called . . . er . . . CW.'

'Curly Wurly!' It was out before I had time to think.

'What?'

'Nickname,' I muttered. 'There's one more sticky,

Gran,' I pointed out.

'Oh, yes. This one's about CW as well. Your dad rang back later and said that Gemma is all upset because CW has gone into a . . . hm.'

'Put your glasses on, Gran,' I suggested.

She didn't seem to hear me.

'It looks like *comma*,' she muttered.

'A coma?'

'Yes, that's *it*,' she said triumphantly. Then her face fell. 'That's bad, eh?'

I suddenly started to sob, right there in the middle of the kitchen with Gran standing there with a bunch of yellow stickies in her hand and her glasses still on top of her head. I sobbed and sobbed and sobbed. It was terrible. I never even trickled out a tear when Gemma had to go to hospital in the middle of the night and there I was bawling my eyes out because this boy I hardly know is in a bad way.

Gran put out her arms to me, but I stepped back. I couldn't bear to be touched.

'Sorry,' I mumbled, and I escaped to my room.

After a while, I stopped blubbing and I told Lucy Fur the good news and the bad news and the worse news. She didn't want to talk about Curly Wurly, but she was not impressed about the miracle drug.

'A million schmillion,' she said, which made me think she must have been watching telly on the sly, because nobody around here ever says things like that. 'I bet if she really needs it, they would have to give it to her and the government would have to pay for it. I don't think you should worry about it, Miranda.'

Yeah, right.

And then she suggested we should get some *chickens*. Lucy Fur is always changing the subject, as a matter of fact. It is a maddening thing about talking bears.

'What on earth would I want chickens for?' I wanted to know, and Lucy Fur said they are very soothing to have around. (She meant good for sad people, but she is quite tactful at times.)

She has a point. We could do with a bit of soothing, in my personal opinion, me and Gran. It is all a bit tense and worried around here at the moment.

It is hard to believe that chickens would be soothing to have around, though, because they are so pecky and sudden, which does not sound soothing at all to me, but then there are the eggs. Maybe I will see what Gran thinks. Since she is my only adult at the moment. Or maybe I won't bother.

I think Gran must be worrying about the million euro because she likes worrying about money – she is always counting it and putting it in little envelopes and hiding them. I am just worrying in a general sort of way about everything. About Gemma. About how come Mum and Dad aren't coming home. About Gran being in charge of me which I don't think is good for me because she is a well-known lunatic. About the million euro, even though Lucy Fur says not to, because I don't really think there is a Nellie's room, and I don't trust the government to pay for it.

And now I have to worry about Curly Wurly too. As if I didn't have enough things to worry about.

Oh, dear! Just when you think things are as bad as they can be, they get worse.

CHAPTER TEN
Pets

Our homework today was to write an essay on My Pet.

'I haven't got a pet,' I told Miss Lucey.

I am not all that into animals, as a matter of fact, though I don't say that out loud, because in my class you are supposed to be, especially if you are a girl, and I just am not all that crazy about them.

But Miss Lucey said, 'What about your famous imagination?'

Which is not a pet, it is just the way my head works.

Then I thought I might write about Lucy Fur, but that is probably not a great idea because if Darren Hoey heard I have a teddy, he'd have me plagued. I'd never live it down.

But I wrote it anyway, because that is what you do if you are at school. They give you homework and you do it, and woe betide you if you don't. I got the idea from Lucy Fur going on about getting chickens.

My Pet

My favourite pets are my chickens. I know it is supposed to be about My Pet, singular, but you can't have only one chicken. I don't know why that is, but maybe they get lonely without their sisters, which I can totally understand. Though it might have to do with the eggs. One egg a day would be enough for me personally, but you can't be always thinking only about yourself.

My chickens are very slim and speckly. You wouldn't know they were chickens, they look more like large dark doves, very smooth, and they do peck, but I am training them to do it gracefully. That is quite hard because chickens are not good at learning, obviously. I can understand now why teachers get annoyed with children. They would wear you out, chickens. They don't listen and they have no interest in learning tricks.

Their eggs are the palest pale, pale pink, like sunset clouds. Very beautiful, in my personal opinion.

I was quite pleased with this because I thought I made it seem as if I really did have chicks even though I haven't. I think that is what Miss Lucey meant about my famous imagination.

I showed it to Gran and I asked her what she thought about the idea of getting chickens like in the essay and she said, 'Jesus, Mary and Joseph, Miranda, do you not think we have enough on our plate without chicks to be looking after?' Which I thought was a bit mean of her because she has Tantum, after all, and I have no pets, so I said, 'Well, I think it's a good idea and I would like that, but nobody ever asks me what I would like around here because I am only a child and I am not even sick.'

'Ah, Miranda,' Gran said.

Whatever that was supposed to mean.

Darren Hoey wrote about a tractor for his pet. I was pretty impressed with that. I was sure he would write about something really obvious like a collie-dog or a goldfish. COR did her rabbit, who is called Bronco and, in my personal opinion, is rather silly. What is the point of a rabbit? I mean, they don't even lay eggs. Except for the Easter Bunny, of course.

I think I might put some chickens in Magnanimous, actually. They can be pets for the police-giraffes. I like the idea of the giraffes daintily picking up their feet to avoid stepping on the chickens. That would give the burglars a chance to get away, which is only fair, considering all the advantages the giraffes have.

That thought made me laugh. You have to laugh, don't you? Because otherwise you would cry. Gran is always saying that. Sometimes, I have to admit, she talks sense.

I wish Gemma was better. I wish Mum and Dad were home. I wish we had a million euro. I wish Curly Wurly would come out of the coma. I wish we could get some chicks.

CHAPTER ELEVEN
Operations

When Mum rang today she had her smiley voice on. It's all twittery like sparrows in a hedge. She always does the twittery, smiley thing when she doesn't want to alarm me. But I knew immediately that something was up, so I asked her what was going on, and she said they have to do an operation on Gemma. Surgery, like. She kept calling it a 'little op', as if it was a puppy or something.

I was dying to know how Curly Wurly was, but I didn't want to ask Mum in case she thought I wasn't worrying enough about Gemma. Which I was *as well*.

I don't know if Gemma's surgery is going to be instead of the million-euro drugs or as well as. Nobody ever explains anything to me. I will try not to think about it until after it is all over. That is the best plan.

That is a thing in my family, as a matter of fact.

People are always scaring the wits out of me by trying not to scare me. They say nothing or if they say something they make it seem all harmless, even when it is obviously not one little bit harmless. Mum was being so smiley and twittery you would think having an operation was a very special kind of treat. I am not terribly keen on operations, as a matter of fact. It gives me the collywobbles just to think about it.

When I was about five, Gran had to have an operation and I got terribly upset at the thought of it and my parents didn't know how to calm me down and they asked my Uncle Frank to explain it to me. He is a big-shot doctor these days, but at the time he was a medical student or maybe a junior doctor and he was also as mad as a hatter. He is not a bit mad any more. I don't know how that happens to people. How can you be all bouncy and giggly and love scaring people one minute and the next thing you go driving around in a Jaguar and wear cufflinks?

So anyway Uncle Frank borrowed a trolley from the canteen in his hospital. Not a wobbly little tea trolley for cakes and cups but one of those big silvery ones with rubber wheels, and one evening he drove it into our kitchen and there was a person-shaped sort of lump on it, only it was covered in a sheet so you couldn't see who was under it. It was like one of those scenes in a morgue on the telly when the distraught parents go to identify their loved one, only I probably didn't think that at the time because I only watched things like *Peppa Pig* and *Bob the Builder* in those days and I certainly didn't know a word like *distraught*. This was long before Word of the Day.

So anyway, Uncle Frank is wearing his white doctory coat and he has one of those liquorice twist things around his neck, only it isn't made of liquorice, it is made of something boring, and he is waving the carving knife around and the bread knife, and the person-shaped lump under the sheet is heaving and muffled splutters are coming out of it and I am *terrified*.

So then Uncle Frank says, 'Now, Miranda, I want to show you how an operation works, so you will understand it and you won't be frightened. Right?'

I nodded, though I was still terrified.

So then Uncle Frank lifts up a corner of the sheet and starts plunging away good-oh with the two knives, and suddenly he shouts, 'Oh, no, would you look at that heart, this will never do, out it comes,' and there is a squeal and there's all blood all over the sheet and this heart comes leaping up into the air and whooshes across the room and lands with a red squelchy plop on the floor and that is when I vomited. It was lucky we were in the kitchen where it is only a plasticky kind of floor, not the best carpet, and next thing Gemma leaps up from the tea trolley and she is streaked with blood and she is yelping and roaring with laughter and patting me on the back and getting a bucket to clean it all up and I am sitting on a chair and there is vomit-flavoured drool hanging from my chin and I am very wobbly and she is saying, 'Oh, Miranda, it was only a joke, come on, cheer up.'

'But your *heart*!' I whimpered, pointing at the sodden red lump on the floor.

Uncle Frank strode over to it and speared it with his bread knife and brought it back to me, dripping blood all the way across the floor.

'It's a pepper, Miranda,' he said, waving it under my nose, and that is what it was, a great big red bell pepper, covered in ketchup. Gemma told me afterwards that they had to dilute the ketchup with water to make it drip properly. I don't know if they do that in the movies.

They all said they were just trying to make a joke out of surgery so I wouldn't be so scared about Gran having an operation, but I didn't think it was a very funny joke, and I have always had a queasy kind of relationship with operations ever since.

Gemma is not afraid of blood the way I am. Maybe if you are always going to hospital you get used to it. Or maybe she is just braver than me. But anyway, she thought the whole operation trick was a great joke and she and Uncle Frank kept bursting out laughing for weeks afterwards, every time they remembered it, but it only made me want to cry.

I started to tell COR that operation story today in school because it is years ago and now I am over it and can see the funny side.

'See, my gran had to have this operation,' I started.

COR put her hand on my arm between the wrist and the elbow, and she said, 'Oh, Miranda, that's dreadful.'

'No, no, no,' I said. 'It was all *ages*—'

But before I could explain how this had been years ago, when I was only small, Miss Lucey came marching in with a big laundry basket full of old clothes. She called them costumes, but they were old clothes. We were going to have a dress rehearsal for our number in the concert. It was kind of fun. School can be OK some of the time.

But the thing is, I never did get to tell COR the Uncle-Frank-and-the-bleeding-heart-operation story.

I didn't realise it at the time, but that was a *calamity*. Because if I'd told COR the story, she wouldn't have so totally got hold of the wrong end of the stick the way she did. But I didn't and she did and last night was the most embarrassing night of my WHOLE LIFE.

CHAPTER TWELVE
A Family Tragedy

The concert was last night.

Darren sang his blackbirdy heart out and the rest of us were all ready to sing our chorus and we were just about to burst into song when suddenly COR stepped out to the front of the stage and she coughed a bit and twisted her hands until everyone in the audience stopped shuffling and chattering and then she cleared her throat and made an announcement. That is what she called it. This is what she said:

Good evening, everyone, I have an announcement to make. We would like to dedicate our part of the concert to our classmate, Miranda Anastasia Maguire.

What! That was me! Why was our song being dedicated to ME? And who had told COR my horrible middle name?

(I hope nobody called Anastasia is reading this and is offended. I think it is a very beautiful name for a person of about forty. But for me, it is just too elegant.)

My head was full of pounding noises and my heart was pumping so hard I thought it was going to leap out of my chest, like the big red pepper that Uncle Frank had sent flying across the room that day he did the pretend operation, and my ears were ringing and all I could see was swimmy colours instead of things and people.

I would have fainted, only luckily Darren had stepped back from the front of the stage for the chorus bit and was behind me, and he caught me by the elbows as I went down and he propped me up and said something into my ear, I don't know what, but whatever it was, it brought me to my senses. (The Darren Project was working. Mysteriously.)

Which is more than can be said for COR. Bad enough that she had revealed to the whole school, the whole town, maybe even the whole county, that my middle name is *Anastasia*, but now she was telling everyone about our Family Tragedy. That is what she was calling

77

it. The Maguire Family Tragedy. It sounds like a rock band, doesn't it, and if I hadn't been feeling so terrible, I might have seen the funny side of it, but there was nothing funny about being up there on the stage, with Darren Hoey just about managing to prevent me from slumping into a trembling heap on the floor, and hearing people muttering and exclaiming about our family. I hate being the centre of attention – unless it is for winning Word of the Day. Other people in my family hate it even more than I do.

I couldn't make out where COR got hold of this idea. She doesn't even know about Gemma being sick. She's been in our house lots of times, she's met Gemma, but you wouldn't know she was sick just by looking. She looks nice, Gemma, in my personal opinion. She's pretty, as a matter of fact.

COR was still babbling on, and I suddenly realised that the Family Tragedy she was telling the nation about had nothing to do with Gemma. It was *Gran* she was talking about. Gran! Gran is many things, but a Tragic Heroine she is not.

I didn't hear exactly what she said, my head was too noisy, but she was yacking away about Gran to everyone in the hall: COR's parents and all her brothers and sisters. Everyone in my school and most of their parents.

My teacher. The principal. The woman in the post office. The librarian. The guy who runs the pub. The caretaker of the town hall who also caretakes the church. Mr and Mrs Hoey and all the little Hoeys. EVERYONE.

And then she put the tin hat on it, my lovely friend Caroline O'Rourke. She ended by saying, 'So we are going to send around a hat for your contributions to this life-saving surgery.'

A hat.

A *HAT*.

Caroline O'Rourke was collecting MONEY for us. OK, so we haven't got a million euro for a wonder-drug for Gemma, but we're not a *charity case*.

I felt another wave of nausea coming over me and I actually leant back against Darren for support. Not moral support, obviously. Just so I wouldn't fall over.

Was nobody going to *stop* her? That's the thing about adults. They are all over the place annoying you when you are being perfectly all right, and then when you need them, they disappear into the woodwork.

The only good thing was that Mum and Dad were in Dublin. Maybe they would never hear about this shameful episode. (Fat chance, but I was clutching at straws.)

The rest of the concert passed in a blur. I was so glad when we were able to get off that stage and hide in our dressing room. But then it got *worse still*.

Gran came storming round to the stage door to pick me up for going home and she was raging. Absolutely raging. With ME! As if I had been the one who stood up there and said all that stuff.

'What have you been *saying*?' she was yell-whispering into my ear, as she held me fiercely by the elbow. (Between Gran and Darren, my elbows are covered in bruises today.) 'And where did you get such a *nonsensical* idea from?'

She was steering me ahead of her now, using my poor elbow like a rudder.

'I didn't say anything, Gran, I didn't, I didn't, I promise I didn't. It was COR's own idea. I don't know what got into her. It is mad. But it's Not My *Fault*.'

'It's all those blinking things you *write*!' Gran hissed. 'You've been filling people's heads with nonsense about our family's private affairs, writing those wretched stories of yours, making people think we are a *case*.'

Me? I don't know anything about our family's private affairs, as a matter of fact. Everything is so private in our family, I don't even know what is going on myself and I am right there in the middle of it with no iPhone. It is so unfair!

'Gran, I *didn't*!' I was whimpering now. 'You have read everything I wrote, and there is nothing private in there. It's all about chicks and Marie Curie and stuff. How did she even know my middle name is Anastasia? *Nobody* knows that.' Except a few grown-ups, I suppose. And Gemma. It is a *secret*.

Gran stopped short. She dropped my elbow. She went a bit red in the face.

'Gran! *You* told Caroline O'Rourke my most closely guarded secret?'

'Eh – no. I didn't exactly *tell* her.'

'You mean, you wrote her a letter about my *name*? Sent her an email, maybe?'

'Of course not. I maybe – eh – let it slip. By mistake.'

'By mistake? You mistakenly told her my middle name. In conversation, like.'

'Well, one day you were looking for your schoolbag or something, and Caroline, she's such a friendly girl, isn't she . . . ?'

Way too friendly, I thought to myself with a glower.

'Well, Caroline was sitting around waiting for you and we got talking and—'

'Gran, I don't need to know all the *details*. You *told* her. End of story.'

'No, I didn't. She worked it out.'

'From something you said, obviously.'

I bet she said I was called after my great-grandmother, Anastasia Davis. Gran is very proud of Anastasia. She has a portrait of her, as a matter of fact, in her real house, over the fireplace. She is an ugly old bag, but having a family portrait makes Gran feel important.

'Just hold on there a minute, young lady,' Gran said. 'You are the one that has told the whole town that I am *dying of lung cancer* and am in urgent need of surgery. I think that's a bit more to the point, actually.'

'*What*?!!!!'

So *that* was what COR had been saying when I was half-fainting and couldn't really hear what was going on. That *Gran* was dangerously ill and needed an operation. Well, at least she hadn't dragged Gemma into it. Which was something. I suppose.

'I am not going to repeat it,' said Gran sulkily. 'It is too embarrassing. And it is NOT TRUE, Miranda. How could you go around telling fibs like that? Is it looking for notice you are? Imagination is all very well and good, but making up stories about other people's health is another thing, so it is. I am *mortified*.'

She had a point, I have to say. Not that it is embarrassing to be sick, obviously, but it is definitely embarrassing if people think you are sick when you are not, *especially* if that makes them feel they have to give you money. It's a funny thing. Money is dead useful and everyone needs it, but it is terribly embarrassing if people feel they should give it to you. I don't know why that is. I will have to have a conversation with Lucy Fur about it.

But it had *nothing to do with me*. I hadn't even properly heard COR saying all that about Gran. I was so fixated on being called Miranda Anastasia Maguire, I think I was deaf with the shock.

Where on earth had COR got that crackpot idea about Gran from? I used to think she didn't have much imagination, but it looks like I was wrong about that. She has *far too much* imagination.

'I *didn't*, Gran. I never said such a thing.'

She didn't believe me. I could tell.

'Well, between you, you and Caroline O'Rourke have created a right hoo-hah, I can tell you. I don't know how I am going to face the people of this town ever again. Plus there is two hundred and seventy-three euro odd in that hat of Caroline's that we have to give back to people. I'd like to know how you are going to work that one out, so I would.'

'Two hundred euro? How do you know?'

'Nearly *three* hundred,' hissed Gran. 'That's how much she'd got before your teacher managed to put a stop to it. Miss Lucey and I counted it. She's keeping it for the moment till they decide what to do with it.'

By now we had reached Gran's car and she had yanked open the passenger door and was pushing me in, as if I was resisting arrest or something.

I am going to personally murder Caroline O'Rourke and then I am never going to be friends with her again.

CHAPTER THIRTEEN
A Conundrum

Of course I did not really mean that about murdering COR. She was trying to be kind. Personally, I think kind people can be a bit of a pain, especially if they are determined to be kind whether you want their help or not. You would be worn out with them. My life is a total mess, and kindness is making it worse.

I had to get to the bottom of it, though, so I asked COR the next day in little break, 'Can you *please* explain to me where you got the idea that my gran was dying of lung cancer and needs an operation?'

'From *you*,' she said.

'*Me*? I never said that. It's not true, so why would I say it?'

COR shrugged. 'You wrote it in your Lung Cancer essay.'

'I did *not!*' I started grubbing about in my schoolbag looking for my English copybook to check that essay.

'You did, you said she had *succumbed.*'

I was leafing furiously through my copy now. And then I found it. I read through it quickly. COR was looking over my shoulder, breathing hotly in my ear.

'There!' she screeched, and she jabbed her fat thumb triumphantly at the last bit:

I have told my gran that and she agrees with me but it is probably too late. She has already succumbed.

'Look!' yelped COR. 'It says she has "succumbed". I asked Miss Lucey what that meant and she said if you succumb to a disease, it means you have died of it or you are about to die of it.'

'That's not what I meant,' I said weakly. 'I only meant—'

'And then only the day before yesterday,' COR was rattling on, 'you told me she needed an operation, and I knew it must be a really hard operation because she was nearly dead already and that would mean it would be very expensive, and I was worried about you all. I knew there was something wrong in your family, you've been all upset lately, and . . .'

She stopped for a moment and I said, 'My gran is not sick, COR. She was in the audience last night. You saw her yourself!'

Nobody could possibly think Gran is sick. She is as tough as an old boot. Though she is a bit old, I suppose. People always think if someone is sick in your family it is probably the oldest person.

'Well, you *did* say she had "succumbed",' said COR. 'You definitely said that.'

'I meant she had succumbed *to cigarettes*.'

'What does *that* mean?'

'It means she has given in to them, they have overcome her, like.' Which they had. At the time.

'Oh!' said COR. Her voice was a little bit apologetic. 'Well . . .'

Then she squinched up her eyes, looking all puzzled. 'But you definitely *said* about her needing an operation. You started to tell me about it the other day.'

'Yes,' I said with a sigh. I wish COR would listen *properly*. 'I was just going to tell you a story about the time my gran needed an operation. It was years ago. When I was *five*. And she had it and it was fine and she has been better for years; she is *as right as rain*. As you know perfectly well. You only have to look at her, you dumb-cluck.'

'Oh,' said COR again. 'I'm sorry.'

'That's all right. It's not your fault,' I said, in my kindest, most dignified voice. I really am a very fine person. 'Not really.'

'All is forgiven?' she asked hopefully

'Not all, no,' I said.

She looked alarmed.

'I forgive you for telling the whole world that my gran is dying of lung cancer, COR. Even though I got into massive trouble with my gran over it.'

'Thanks,' she said breathlessly.

'I find it harder to forgive you, though, for telling the whole world that my family needs a *collection* to pay for an operation for my gran. But I do forgive you for that too. You meant well.'

'Yeah,' she said, cheering up. 'I did.'

'But I cannot forgive you for telling the world that my middle name is – is – well, what it is.'

'But it's a lovely name,' said COR. 'That's why I mentioned it. It makes you sound grown-up and elegant.'

'Which I am not,' I said. 'But, look, COR, you are going to have to give the money back or my gran is going to come around and chop your fingers off.'

COR immediately sat on her hands.

'That's a joke,' I said. 'But she *is* IMMENSELY cross.'

If COR had collected a million euro, I might have been tempted to hang onto it. Two hundred and seventy-something euro is in a different category, though. It may sound like an awful lot of money, but it is only an awful lot of money if you are buying sweets. It is not an awful lot of money if you are buying medicine, and it is not going to get us very far with that miracle drug for Gemma, so we may as well give it back.

I don't know how COR is going to do that. It is a conundrum. There are far too many mysteries, riddles and conundrums in my life, as a matter of fact.

CHAPTER FOURTEEN
Hens With Dentures

Something miraculous has happened. It is just as well, because I was getting very depressed what with public humiliation and Mum and Dad being away and Gran being bonkers and also very cross with me. It is so miraculous that I had to tell Gemma about it, so I got some card and I took a photo of Joseph on my gran's mobile phone and I printed it out and I wrote a very special get-well card for her.

You will be wondering who Joseph is. I have been keeping that as a surprise. You can read all about it now in the big long message I wrote to Gemma, and All Will Be Revealed. It is a very good miracle, I think you will agree, but it is hard to know whether I made it happen with my writing or whether it really was the Tooth Fairy.

Dear Gemma

I invented an ice knife for your operation, but it is not patented yet, so you will just have to make do with the ordinary ones. The thing about ice ones is that they don't hurt, they just cut and melt and there is
no blood.

The picture is of Joseph, who is a new pet in this house. I don't know how I am going to keep her safe from Tantum Ergo, but I have made a cage for her and her sisters (there are three of them), only when it is chicks you call it a coop. I made it out of chicken wire, which is very logical when you think about it, and it is in the garage, where Tantum never goes because it is too cold for him. Gran has gone to town on her bicycle to buy an infrared light to keep the chicks warm. As long as Tantum Ergo doesn't find out they should be all right. If you are reading this when you wake up from your operation, it is OK, you are not hallucinating, it is all true.

And if you hear a weird story from here about Gran having cancer, that is all lies. Or not lies exactly. More a misunderstanding, so please don't believe it if you hear it and I will explain it all later.

Love from your best sis, M xx

PS in case you are worrying there is also straw or maybe it is hay, I am never sure about that, and of course food. For the chicks. In the garage.

PPS Darren Hoey was Oliver in the concert because his voice is so mellifluous like a blackbird. That is also true and not a hallucination, though I don't blame you if you think it is. COR thought blackbirds are the same as crows and make an awful rackety noise. I had a big job explaining
to her that a blackbird is a particular kind of bird, not just any bird that happens to be black. I had to show her on the internet as that was the only way she would believe me and it was not very satisfying because she just tossed her head anyway, even though I was RIGHT and she said 'Oh, well, who cares?'

I care.

PPPS: How are you getting on with Treasure Island? Have they found treasure?

PPPPS: I wasn't going to mention this because I am not sure if I am supposed to know about it but Gran told me that CW is really bad and I

am very sorry and I won't write any more
because it will make me cry. If he wakes up will
you give him my love. If that's all right.

So that is the miracle. Those chicks I wrote about for school last week have actually materialised, right in our house. Three of them, just like I wrote for My Pet. Three tiny black chicks with little fluffs of white. Gran said the Tooth Fairy brought them, which is ridiculous, in my personal opinion, because that is not the kind of thing the Tooth Fairy does, though I have to admit that my tooth has finally disappeared from my bedside table. I am suspicious, however.

People do talk about hens' teeth, though, which means something very rare, so maybe the Tooth Fairy might keep chickens and that is why she needs all the teeth, I don't know for sure. It is a good idea, even if it is not true: hens with dentures. So then she might have some leftover chicks and that is why she brought them to me. It is a bit of a stretch, though, to believe all that. I'm just saying.

They are only small, the chicks, cutesy little handfuls of fluff, so there will be no eggs for ages. I wonder if the eggs could possibly be cloud pink? That really would be a miracle.

I was wondering what to call them and then I remembered what Gran said when I asked her if we could maybe get chicks so I decided to call them Jesus, Mary and Joseph, even though they are all girls.

I have no idea how you can tell that they are girls, but Gran says there is a job called a chicken-sexer.

I told COR that and she said that was gross and that if she said the word 'chicken-sexer' in her house, someone would smack her.

I said, 'It's not as gross as it sounds, COR. It only means a person whose job is to work out which chicks are male and which are female.'

'That's still gross,' COR said, 'because, I mean, *how* do they do that?'

'There's probably a machine for it. Measuring hormones or something.'

'*Hormones*?' squealed COR. 'Ewww!'

'They're only chemicals,' I said. 'You don't need to be so squeamish.'

'But why do they need to do that?' COR asked.

'So you know which ones are going to lay eggs when they grow up, you dumb-cluck. Only the girl ones will lay eggs when they are older. Obviously.'

'Obviously,' she echoed, though I could tell that thought had never crossed her mind.

I invited COR over to see the chicks after school. She fell totally in love with them, which is not surprising, because they are *divine*.

Gran wants to rename the first chick Judy because she says we are not in Spain and you can't call a chick by the Holy Name. Apparently anyone can have that name in Spain, it doesn't count as so holy there.

'You called your cat after a hymn,' I said.

'That's different,' she said. Which grown-ups are always saying.

But Judy is a big comedown from Jesus, so I am not going to let Gran get away with that. Not after she humiliated *me* by telling COR my secret middle name. You might think that was COR's fault, but if Gran hadn't told her, she wouldn't have been able to do it so it was definitely mostly Gran's fault.

'Where did you get the chicks?' COR asked, watching delightedly as Joseph went darting about on the kitchen table. 'Did you buy them yourself? Where's your sister, by the way? I haven't seen her for ages.'

'She's in Dublin,' I said airily. It's true, but it is not, of course, the whole truth. 'Gran bought the chicks, though she is letting on the Tooth Fairy brought them. I think she is feeling guilty. Like, you know, when criminals do a bad thing and then they have to do something nice for the person they have damaged.'

'What is your gran feeling guilty about?'

'About telling someone someone else's secret name, and the first someone telling the whole world about it and embarrassing the second someone to *bits*.'

'Oh,' said COR, and she went red.

'Or,' I went on, 'it could also be a miracle. The arrival of the chicks, I mean.'

'A miracle?'

COR wouldn't be one for miracles.

'Something impossible but you can still imagine it and then it really happens. Like Darren catching me before I fainted.'

'Ah, Darren's all right,' she said. 'Ever since he can sing and Miss Lucey said he was a blackbird, he has found out that being nice to people makes them like you.'

Now *there's* a miracle. Caroline O'Rourke saying something friendly about Darren Hoey. What is the world coming to?

My favourite chick is Joseph because she cheeps the loudest and looks a bit frightened, and that is why she is the one I photographed for Gemma. Of course I didn't say anything to Gemma about the collection for Gran's operation, because she would be dead embarrassed in case people thought *she* was the one having the operation (even though that is true, or might be true or might be going to be true). I didn't mention anything either about how they all heard I am called Anastasia on my birth certificate, because that is between me and the Registrar of Births, Deaths and Marriages and NOBODY ELSE and I wish they would all just forget about it.

CHAPTER FIFTEEN
The Bacteria Farm

Mum rang this morning from the hospital and she wasn't doing the twittery voice any more. The opposite, in fact. She sounded all flat and floppy, like a balloon someone had let the air out of. I used to hate the twittery voice because it sounded all silly and kind of cringe-making, like a little kid doing pirouettes to show off, but I have to say I found the flat-balloon voice even worse.

The thing is, Gemma is not going to get her operation after all. That sounded like great news to me, because I hate even the *thought* of operations, but apparently it is not good news at all. The reason she can't have the operation, Mum says, is that she is not well enough. I know, that sounds mad, so I will say it again just to be clear: Gemma is not well enough to have that operation.

Isn't that weird? I mean, operations are supposed to

make you better, but you only get better if you are sick in the first place, so of course you have to be sick to *need* an operation, so how come you have to be *well* to have one? Duh?

I asked Mum that on the phone but she didn't understand the question. That could be because she is stupid or it could be because I didn't ask it very clearly. I don't much like either of those explanations, as a matter of fact.

All she kept saying was, 'She has an infection. It is a very bad one. So they can't operate.' And she was snivelling. I can understand why, but it is very hard to have a sensible phone conversation with a person who is snivelling.

That did kind of make sense, because Gemma told me once that she is a bacteria farm. That made me laugh because it is a funny way to put it, and I do think she meant it as a kind of joke, but it is actually quite a good way of explaining it. It means you have to be in isolation, which is a kind of hospital version of solitary confinement, so it is not all that funny if you're the one who is the bacteria farm.

I wish my mum and dad were here so I could ask them more about it, but I am stuck with Gran. Anyway, they wouldn't tell me even if they were at home. That is the thing about life around here at the moment, nobody is telling me anything and horrible things are happening and the more they happen, the more nobody talks about it. Especially not to me. Unless they have to. Like about the operation not going ahead. They had to tell me that or I would be asking annoying questions, and they don't like that.

I take that back about being stuck with Gran. She is doing her best. She was great about the chicks, and I think she has forgiven me about COR's announcement. (Not that I need to be forgiven. I didn't do *anything*.) But it is not the same as the family all being properly together and Gemma being all right, the way things usually are.

I used to wish I lived in a normal family where nobody is always sick. But now I just wish we could go back to our normal level of not-normal.

I was discussing miracles this evening with Lucy Fur, who is quite an intellectual bear.

'So first there was Gran giving up smoking,' I said.

Lucy was quite impressed with that. She didn't know about it. I forgot to tell her at the time.

'Then there were the chicks that arrived from the Tooth Fairy,' I said.

Allegedly, said Lucy Fur. She is a stickler for accuracy.

'Allegedly,' I agreed.

So why don't you try doing something about that bacteria farm? Lucy Fur suggested when I told her that part.

'How do you mean?'

Sometimes Lucy is a bit *too* intellectual.

Well, you could try stamping them out, she said.

'Stamping what out?'

The bacteria, dumb-cluck.

I do not take kindly to being called 'dumb-cluck', as a matter of fact, but Lucy Fur has no respect for my sensitivities.

'How could I do that?'

In Magnanimous of course, said Lucy, as if it was the most obvious thing in the world. Which it certainly is not. Who would ever think of using Fantasy Geography to cure severe bacterial infections? Only a talking bear.

And then she yawned and went to sleep. She can be quite a maddening bear at times.

I stayed awake and thought confusing thoughts for a while and then I decided to make a Table of Miracles, to help get the thoughts all straight in my head, and this is the table and I am quite proud of it:

Describe miracle	Who made it happen	Observations
The people who went to sea in a sieve, they did, in a sieve they went to sea – and they weren't drowned.	Edward Lear, old-timer poet	It only happened in a poem so it is not really real.
Miracles of Modern Medicine	Scientists, surgeons, pharmacologists	Sometimes they work, sometimes they don't.
Cures at Lourdes	Holy Mary	Ditto
Gran gave up the cigarettes.	I wrote about it in one of my essays.	I suspect I have miraculous powers.
Lucy Fur can talk.	I just made that up.	But it is a secret.
Darren Hoey turns out to have a mellifluous voice.	This happened all by itself.	The world is a miraculous kind of place.
Darren was nice to me when I nearly fainted in the concert when COR told everyone my secret middle name.	I did say I was going to do a Darren Project to make Darren nice.	To be honest, I only really thought it up, I didn't actually write it in an essay or anything, so I may not have personally caused this miracle.
Chicks arrived out of nowhere.	Possibility (a) The Tooth Fairy brought them. Possibility (b) Gran secretly got them for me. Possibility (c) I wrote about them in an essay and that made the miracle.	Possibility (c) is my favourite explanation.
Ice knives for operations, which don't hurt	I wrote about this in Fantasy Geography and then it turns out that there really are lasers in the world. Gran told me about them.	I am not sure if this is a miracle or not, but it is a very good thing anyway.
Cloud pink eggs from black-and-white speckled chickens	Hasn't happened yet.	Fingers crossed.
Gemma's infection gets cured.	I am going to write about this in Fantasy Geography and see if it works.	Toes crossed too.

This is what I wrote for the bacteria-curing miracle:

The Bacteria Farm

So there is this Bacteria Farm in Magnanimous. It is a long way from the city, way out in the middle of the bog, where people can't get infected by it. But still, a Bacteria Farm is not a good thing to have on an inhabited island and all the people were wondering what could be done about it, because the inhabitants of Magnanimous are caring people. By and large.

The Very Tallest Giraffe, who is, of course, the Chief of Police, decided that the best solution would be if all the police-giraffes mounted an attack on the Bacteria Farm. Not to destroy the farm itself, just to stamp out all the bacteria. So he deployed all his troops, every last giraffe of them, and off they went out onto the bog to stamp out the bacteria.

I asked Lucy Fur what she thought of that, when she eventually woke up, and she was rather dubious.

It sounds a bit too easy, she said at last.

'Does it have to be hard?' I asked.

I'd say miracles are hard enough to pull off, she said.

So it was back to the drawing board.

At first it all went swimmingly. The giraffes had a great time kicking up their heels and they did manage to stamp out quite a lot of the bacteria with their big clumpy giraffey feet.

But after a while, the bacteria started to fight back, and instead of taking all that stamping lying down, they took up residence in the giraffes' hooves and now the giraffes have footrot, which is a distant relation to tommyrot but a lot more painful.

So now the giraffes have to stay out on the Bacteria Farm because they have to be in isolation in case they give the footrot to everyone else. The Very Tallest Giraffe had to send some people out with cherry-pickers to feed them, because there are no trees out there on the Bacteria Farm and the giraffes will not get better unless they are well fed and their immune systems are kept topped up.

We know all about immune systems in this house because of Gemma needing to keep her strength up. It's this weird combination of carbohydrates and health food around here and not much chocolate. Or not for me anyway.

Lucy Fur had a read of that and she thought it had potential.

'Miracle potential?' I asked.

Mmm, said Lucy non-committally, *but there is another problem now*.

So I asked her what that was.

Well, look, the police force is all out on the Bacteria Farm fighting infection. This is not a great idea. Imagine what must be happening back in Splendiferous.

She's right, of course. She usually is. This writing business is more complex than you'd think.

So I have decided that what is going on back in Splendiferous is that the burglars have gone crazy because there are no police and they are shinning up drainpipes and mugging people for their mobile phones and there is chaos, chaos everywhere. I am going to have to think of something or the whole of Splendiferous is going to be overrun by a criminal element and then the ordinary people who are not burglars are going to want to have guns to protect themselves and that never ends well.

I asked Uncle Frank about that once, as a matter of fact, because it is kind of hard to get your head around.

'Why is it such a bad idea for people to have guns?' I asked him.

And he said, 'Because if the good guys get guns then

they are bad guys.'

'That is mad,' I said. 'They are just good guys with guns.'

And he said, 'No, the fellow with the gun is always the bad guy.'

'How come?' I said.

He shrugged and said, 'Guns are like that. That is just the way it works. Except maybe for hunting rifles. Which are all right, in their place, as long as you are not a pheasant.'

I thought I kind of saw what he meant, but at the same time it didn't make total sense. Like life, really.

'But what if they both had guns?' I said. 'The good guys *and* the bad guys?'

And he said, 'That is what you call war, Miranda.'

Which means that *now* I have to find a way to get the giraffes cured of the footrot so they can come back to Splendiferous and keep the burglars under control and prevent war from breaking out.

I am getting a bit distracted now from writing a miracle for Gemma, but I can't have war breaking out in Magnanimous, in my personal opinion. War is not the kind of thing that is supposed to happen in Magnanimous. It is supposed to be an Island of Peace and Wellbeing, like one of those shops that sells crystals and incense and those things you hang in trees to make a chiming sound in the wind.

The Very Tallest Giraffe has called in Marie Curie, the Rhyming Scientist, to solve the footrot problem, because she is good at curing things. (That is why she is called Curie, as a matter of fact.)

Dr Curie thought long and hard about the problem and then she put in a Purchase Order for a good few buckets of medicine for the giraffes' feet.

'We need a lot of buckets,' she wrote on the Purchase Order, 'and they need to be good and big, and the giraffes have to stand in the buckets for a fair while so that their feet are well soaked in the medicine.'

'This will cost millions of doubloons,' observed the Very Tallest Giraffe.

'That is not my affair,' said Marie Curie the Rhyming Scientist. 'You will just have to send around a hat.'

So the Very Tallest Giraffe took off his very own extra tall helmet and gave it to the Next Tallest Giraffe to start a doubloon collection.

Doubloons are the kind of money they have in Magnanimous, by the way. I did not make that word up. It is pirate money and they have it in books like *Treasure Island*, I believe. It is a very fine word, in my personal opinion, but the meaning is not all that interesting so I did not make it a Word of the Day. Instead I did 'cherry-picker', which is a less beautiful word but a more interesting idea. In my personal opinion.

CHAPTER SIXTEEN
The F-Word

We were expecting Mum and Dad home today, and I was dying for them to come because I want to show them Jesus, Mary and Joseph, and I was also wondering if maybe the Bacteria Farm thing had worked and cured Gemma's infection. That would be the *best* miracle. Also if Curly Wurly woke up. That would be the second best.

So I was quite excited when the phone rang. I was in my room and I heard it ringing in the kitchen and I came out to answer it, because I thought it might be Mum or Dad to say what time they would be home. They often do that. They ring from the car to say they will be home in twenty minutes. They have been away for more than a week at this stage, and Lucy Fur is kicking up an awful fuss about it. She says I should write it in the Book of Neglect.

Trust Lucy Fur to remember the Book of Neglect. That is a thing I used to do when I was younger. I had this special black notebook and I used to write down all the mean things my parents did to me. And not just the mean-on-purpose things, but also things like cancelling my birthday party. (That only happened once and it was one of the times that Gemma had to be whisked off to hospital in a hurry.) Or not signing my homework notebook (which is very embarrassing because it makes the teachers suspicious). Or not coming to my school concert. (That happened twice, as a matter of fact.) Or . . . I'd better stop or I will make myself cross. I tore up the Book of Neglect ages ago and vowed to be a Better Daughter and a Better Sister and not be making myself miserable. It is bad enough when other people make you miserable without making *yourself* miserable as well.

The phone had stopped ringing before I reached the kitchen, so I knew Gran had got it. But when I opened the kitchen door, she slammed the phone down and swung around on her heel and gave me an accusing look as if I had been spying on her or something.

'Who was that?' I asked

Though I knew perfectly well it had to have been Mum or Dad, and it didn't look good. Maybe they weren't coming home after all.

'What?' said Gran, pretending to be distracted. She was playing for time. 'Oh, that. On the phone?'

'Obviously,' I said tartly. (That might be my Word of the Day tomorrow. It has nothing to do with the kind of tarts you eat.)

'Mind your own business,' Gran snapped.

'It *is* my business,' I said, because by now I was sure it had been Mum or Dad, and it wasn't about what time they would be home at. 'This is my house. If the phone rings, I think I am entitled to know who it is.'

That is not exactly true. And of course it isn't exactly my house either. But anyway.

'Ever heard of privacy?' Gran said crankily.

'Certainly I have heard of it,' I said. 'But will you please stop beating about the bush, Gran, and come out with it. What is wrong? Is Gemma worse?'

Gran gave a gasp. 'No,' she said.

That didn't square with the gasp so I didn't believe her. I raised my eyebrows and waited for her to continue. It was very tense. I wish people would just tell me stuff and I didn't have to poke it out of them with a pointy stick. It would wear you out.

'She's a lot better, actually,' Gran went on.

Aha, I thought, *that'd be the miracle*. I was starting to feel the tension lifting just a bit.

'They are going to be able to operate after all.'

I could feel a grin stretching across my face. I never thought I'd be *pleased* to hear about anyone in my family having an operation.

'Tomorrow, probably,' Gran was saying. 'Which means she will have to miss the funeral. *Oh!*'

She clapped her hand across her mouth. She obviously hadn't meant to mention the F-word in front of me.

My smile collapsed. My vision blurred. My knees went wobbly.

At first I thought Gemma must be dead, but then I realised that was ridiculous. You can't miss your own funeral, especially not if it is because you are in theatre getting an operation done on you.

Then I thought wildly (hopefully) that maybe it might be just a pet. Maybe someone's white mouse or goldfish, something small like that that dies a lot, because I wouldn't like to think of someone's actual *dog* dying. But then I realised that was stupid too, because I don't think Gran would be upset about a goldfish that died in Dublin. And Gran was clearly upset.

The next thing I thought was it had to be Mum or Dad. Or both of them. They must have been killed in a car crash. That was *terrible*! There was a Maguire Family Tragedy after all. Poor Gemma. Who was going to look after her now? And poor me too. I burst into tears. Obviously. Anyone would.

Gran had put the heel of her hand to her forehead, just between the eyebrows, and she was making sobbing noises but she wasn't actually crying because there were no tears. We stood like that for a few moments, facing each other across the kitchen, me bawling crying and her making these weird gasping noises. And then I swung around and ran to my own room and banged the door.

Lucy Fur said I was too emotional for conversation but she would just say one thing and that was, *I know you think nobody tells you anything, Miranda, but, look, if your parents were killed in a car crash, someone would have to tell you, wouldn't they? I mean, you would notice. Like, eventually.*

Which is true. I suppose. She's right. It couldn't be that.

So I got over myself and I washed my face and tidied myself up as best I could and then I went back to the kitchen to see what I could get out of Gran. It would wear you out, all this mystery.

She was sitting at the kitchen table with her head in her hands. She looked up when I came in and I said, 'Gran, please tell me who is dead, because I know it is not a goldfish.'

She gave a panicky little giggle at that.

I said, 'This is getting ridiculous, Gran. I know someone has died and everyone is upset and I need to know or I will be imagining terrible things.'

'God bless us and save us,' she said. She was playing for time again, I could tell.

'Don't give me that old Mrs Davis stuff,' I said sternly.

So then she changed tack. 'Merciful hour,' she said.

I wasn't going to stand for that. I waited.

'Well, the way it is, Miranda . . .' she said.

'The way it is, Gran?'

'Well, you know yourself.'

'I do *not*.'

'No, I mean, you know the way all those young ones and young fellas above in the hospital see each other all the time, they are all coming and going, like, sometimes they are sick and sometimes they are well.'

'Yes,' I said. 'I know all that. But WHO is dead?'

'Joshua,' said Gran. 'A lad Gemma was . . . eh . . . friends with.'

'Oh!' I said, and now I was the one clapping my hand over my mouth.

Curly Wurly! That was just *awful*.

It's not as if we were great pals or anything, I mean, I only met him a couple of times, but nobody I knew had ever died before. I didn't really know that lad that went to America and died later. But I did know Curly Wurly, and I liked him. I felt all hollowed out, like an empty nutshell.

I did not want him to be dead. It was all wrong.

'He *died*?' I said. I could hardly believe it. 'Josh? But he's only fifteen, Gran.'

I could feel my bottom lip trembling and my nose fizzing.

I was sorry now I had laughed so much about how cross my Scrabble word had made him that time. Zealous. It's not like it's my fault, obviously, but I wish that hadn't happened. That is the thing about death. It makes you feel grumpy with yourself.

'His poor mother,' said Gran, shaking her head. 'Her lovely son.'

That made me think about his curls.

'Did he have, like, any sisters?' I asked in a tiny voice.

Gran didn't know that. That is the thing about life. Everyone thinks of the mother, which you can kind of understand, but nobody even *knows* if there is a sister.

I texted Gemma later.

Feeling sad about
Curly Wurly?
Me too. M xxx

I wanted to wish her luck tomorrow, for the operation, but it seemed wrong to put that in the same text, so I didn't say anything.

She got back straight away.

Sad. Bad. Mad.
Thx sis.
G

It must be horrible for Gem.

I suppose Mum and Dad are going to the funeral. Gemma would probably like them to do that, since she can't go herself. Also they are waiting for Gemma's operation to be over, so they won't be home just yet. I wish . . .

I am not even going to tell Lucy Fur all that or she will be wanting me to begin a new Book of Neglect. Talking bears are all very well but they don't always know what is appropriate.

Oh, poor old Curly Wurly. And poor old Gemma. It is all just awful.

CHAPTER SEVENTEEN
The Milky Bar Miracle

Yesterday was the worst day I can remember in my whole life. You would think that when you have a really horrible day that maybe the next day might be not so bad. But the thing is, when a person dies, they are still dead the next day, so that is not much of an improvement.

And then other things were not very nice either.

First off, my best miracle is spoilt. I caught Gran smoking again. She does it in the garage. She will kill those poor chicks stone dead with her toxic smoke. I wish Mum would come home and tell her not to do it. I suppose she is feeling tense about Gemma's operation. (I am half-tempted to take up smoking myself, as a matter of fact. No, I'm not, that is a joke.) But even so. There is no point in two people in this family being sick. One is enough in any house.

And then, well, I am not going to go into the details, but Darren Hoey actually won Word of the Day for the second time in the history of education. His word was 'magnanimous'.

I didn't mind so much when he stole 'tommyrot', but 'magnanimous' really hurt. I felt cold in my stomach about it. I feel like quitting school. Only COR says if you do that the guards come and arrest your parents, and I would not like that to happen, especially not with Gemma and everything. It's probably not true, but I wouldn't like to take the risk. Though it would probably be Gran who would be arrested, since she is in charge. Hm, tempting.

COR won Word of the Day yesterday, actually. That is two days in a row when I didn't win. The teacher thought COR had been 'so clever'.

Words of the Day
by Caroline O'Rourke

VERDANT, VERMILION

I have put these two words together because they are both colours and easy to mix up. Verdant means green, but also leafy. Vermilion means a kind of bright orangey red. Ver-y confusing.

That last bit was the clever part, apparently. Ho-ho. The reason I don't think that is a good Word of the Day is because she actually makes you mix up two words you might never have mixed up if she hadn't pointed out how confusing they are. It may be clever but I don't think it is in the spirit of the thing. I am getting tired of other people winning Word of the Day, as a matter of fact.

But then a weird thing happened. Nice weird, but still weird. Darren Hoey gave me a Milky Bar at lunchtime. Just like that. He came up to me in the schoolyard and handed it to me.

'What's that for?' I asked him.

'You,' he said.

'But what is it *for*?' I asked him.

'Eating,' he said. Helpful boy that he is.

'But . . .'

'Just,' he said, and he walked away.

What is *that* all about? Maybe he still thinks that my gran is dying of cancer and that makes him feel sorry for me. But would you give someone a Milky Bar because you think their gran is going to die? Probably not, but then you are not Darren Hoey.

I told COR about it, and I asked her if she thought it was a miracle, and she said it probably was. We shared the Milky Bar. Mustn't look a gift horse in the mouth.

Though maybe he is sorry for having stolen my most important and favourite word ever, 'magnanimous'. That is probably it. It is like blood money, that Milky Bar. He did it to make up to me for being so mean. But it still tasted good.

CHAPTER EIGHTEEN
Young Pups

Gran came and picked me up from school today. Usually I walk home, so I don't know why she thought I needed a lift today. It is not raining or anything. I hate going in the car with her, because she is the world's worst driver. Every journey is a personal tour of vengeance on young pups. For years I thought there must be a puppy farm near our school, she went on so much about young pups, but it turns out that (a) 'young pup' is a thing old people say to describe rude young people and (b) 'young pup' is also Gran Speak for anybody more than two years younger than herself who has the cheek to drive a car on the same road as her.

'How was school?' she asked as we drove off with a screech of tyres, spraying a fountain of mud over Darren Hoey's mum.

'Gran, you have spattered Alice Hoey. She's mud from top to *toe!*'

'Suits her,' said Gran with a grimace.

I felt a bit sorry for Darren's mum. Even though she is to blame for Darren even existing. Though Darren is not the worst. After all, there was the Milky Bar.

'Gran?' I said then.

'Hmmm,' she said. She didn't sound very encouraging.

'Any news?' I asked. 'From the hospital.'

'Oh, yes,' said Gran.

'And?'

'She had the operation.'

'It's *over*?'

'That's what "had" means, Miranda. Past tense.'

'And is she OK?'

It was like drawing teeth. No, not with a pencil. *Pulling* teeth.

'Still asleep, I believe.'

'Gran?' I said.

'Hmm?'

'Is Gemma going to *die*?'

'Of course,' she said, which was not very tactful of her, I have to say, but, look, this is Gran we are talking about.

Then she rolled down the window and yelled, 'Young

pup!' at Dora Carney's dad, who is at least forty-five.

'Gran!' I shouted.

'Well, he never indicated,' she said, fuming. 'He just waltzed out in front of me.'

You really could not imagine Dora Carney's dad waltzing, it is too ridiculous. His tummy looks as if he has a pillow under his jumper and his legs are like tree stumps.

'No,' I said. 'I mean about Gemma. So the operation was a failure?'

'I never said that.'

'Well, you said she was going to *die*.' The words were sticking in my mouth.

'We all die, Miranda,' Gran said firmly, 'and if that Dan Carney has his way you and I will be dead before teatime.'

'Gran, will you please answer the question. Nobody is telling me anything. Is – Gemma – going – to – DIE?'

'I did answer it,' Gran said.

I gulped.

'She is going to die, but not yet.'

There she was again with her we're-all-going-to-die nonsense. Of course we are, but that is not the point.

I slouched in my car seat and made farting noises with my hands. There is a way you can twist your palms together and it works quite well if your hands are a bit sweaty. Darren Hoey showed me.

Gran made a face but said nothing.

When we reached our house, I said, 'So was the operation a success?'

'Hard to say,' said Gran. 'Too soon.'

'But could she get whatever Josh had?'

'I suppose so.'

I gave a little gasp.

'But things affect people differently, Miranda. What can lay one person flat out could give someone else a bit of a sniffle.'

'Oh, Gran, I wish you would say something clear!' I practically yelled.

'Well, it's not clear, Miranda. It's not like algebra. You can't just do the sum and come up with the answer.'

Algebra. I don't even *do* algebra. I am way too young for that particular form of torture.

'But I'd say she'll outlive Tantum Ergo anyway,' Gran said.

Which is useless, because Tantum Ergo is an *old* cat.

She is totally impossible and should probably be shot. (Gran, not Tantum.) I don't care what Uncle Frank says.

CHAPTER NINETEEN
Tantrum

Mum came home from Dublin this evening.

I heard the car coming up the drive and I thought, *Oh, brill, Mum and Dad are home at last, to rescue me from the clutches of the crazed grandmother.* My heart did a little dance. My heart hasn't done much dancing lately. Now at last I might get to hear what was really going on and we would all get to have a proper conversation and I could hear how Gemma really is and I could ask about the funeral, and everything that had been spinning around in my head for the past few days could finally settle down and stop making me so dizzy.

We had just finished dinner when she came in, and I had my map of Magnanimous out and I had all my colouring pencils and markers and things out too and I was drawing in a wishing well. I saw one in a book at school and it looked very pretty, all flowers growing up the arch and three gorgeous peacocks strutting around it. Well, it was a still picture, you couldn't actually see the strutting happening, but still, you knew they were strutters. From the cut of them, as Gran says.

I looked up and saw Mum and I was just about to say 'Hi' to her and Dad when I realised there was no Dad. She was on her own.

My heart decided to sit out the next dance. Mum looked awful. Really exhausted. Her face looked as if it had fallen in on itself and her eyes were all pinkish. I felt quite sorry for her.

It is not exactly that I prefer Dad. You are not allowed to have a favourite parent. It is the same as how parents are supposed to love all their children equally. Though sometimes I would have to say I question that around here. I wouldn't say that out loud, though. Obviously. But the truth is, Dad is better company than Mum, in my personal opinion. So I was kind of disappointed that it was only Mum, but I stood up so I could go and give her a welcome-home kiss.

But Gran jumped up too and she got to Mum first and they hugged and hugged and hugged. I never saw them hugging before. Anyone would think it was Mum's son that had died. You'd never guess she has a perfectly good daughter standing there waiting for a nod or a smile or a hello or . . . just . . . *anything*.

After a while the hug stopped. Well, you can't hug for ever, you would be smothered or die of starvation or something.

And I said, 'Very well, thank you for asking. And you?'

All right, so that was a bit snarky, but I have been here for weeks (well, close enough) with only Gran for company. And Lucy Fur, but she doesn't count. No, she doesn't. Don't be arguing. She is only a teddy.

So then Mum flopped onto a chair and finally she said, 'Hello, Miranda. How did the concert go?'

You might think that was nice of her, interested and all, but she knows how the concert went, or she should know. I told her all about it on the phone the other day, but I let that pass.

'Would you like to meet Jesus, Mary and Joseph?' I asked.

'I don't do saints,' she said wearily. Which is totally untrue. She is always bribing St Anthony.

'They are chicks,' I said. 'Not saints. They are in the garage. I told you about them.'

'Miranda, pet, I would love to meet your friends, but I cannot do anything that would involve getting out of this chair at this moment.'

I hate being called 'pet'.

'They are not my friends,' I said through gritted teeth. I had told her about them at least twice on the phone.

'What?' Mum asked, as if I had said something totally ridiculous, as if she and I lived on different planets, almost as if she had never even met me before.

'THEY ARE NOT MY FRIENDS.

THEY ARE **NOT** MY FRIENDS.

THEY. ARE. NOT. MY. FLAMING. *FRIENDS*!'

Well, you've worked it out. I lost it. You can tell that from all the capital letters. They represent screaming and shouting and yelling. There was also foot-stamping and arm-flailing and hair-pulling (I mean, I pulled my own hair, not Mum's) and tears and, I am sorry to say, a certain amount of snot. I even threw a cup I found handy on the table. It crashed against the wall and shattered.

I am not proud of having thrown a tantrum (and a cup). Obviously. I didn't exactly do it *for effect*. I didn't plan it. I didn't even really do it on purpose. It just came howling and raging out. I didn't do anything to stop it, is all.

Nobody ever listens to me.

Mum sat completely still all through it, as if she were glued to her chair. Her eyes were all glassy as if she were not a real person but a model of herself. And no matter how much I wept and screamed and roared and sobbed, she kept just sitting and staring. I wanted to SHAKE her.

In the end I stopped, of course. You get tired. Your chest hurts and your ribs ache and you are trembling and you have to stop so you can breathe properly.

When I had completely stopped, Gran patted my face all over with a damp facecloth and then she helped me up off the floor (because of course that is where I had ended up) and sat me on a chair and she brushed out my hair and put it in a ponytail for me. She gave me a glass of water.

And then she put her two arms around me and she held me really, really, really tight until I thought my bones were going to get crushed. I didn't hug her back. I couldn't because my arms were pinned in against my body in Gran's grip. She smelt of cigarette smoke. But it felt kind of nice. I think there needs to be more hugging around here, as a matter of fact.

After that I said sorry to Gran and sorry to Mum and Mum said sorry to me and it was fairly civilised and Mum told us all about how terrible a week it had been but she finished by saying that Gemma was very good after her operation and the doctors were saying she would be able to come home in a short while.

She didn't mention Curly Wurly. Neither did I. I just couldn't *bear* to.

So we talked a bit about Gemma and the operation and what the doctors had said and how she was feeling now and how long they thought it would be before she could come home and all this kind of thing. Then I asked Mum about the million-euro drug and I asked her what we were going to do about that, and she said not to worry about it and I thought I was going to *explode* all over again. I probably would have, only I didn't have the energy for it.

Gran must have known I was very nearly going to explode again, because she said to Mum, 'I think maybe it would be a good idea to explain that to Miranda.'

'Oh,' said Mum, and she put down her tea cup. 'Of course. I just meant—'

'Mum!' I couldn't stand it much longer. 'Just tell me.'

'Well, Miranda, that drug isn't suitable for Gemma,' Mum said.

'Oh!' I said. I didn't know how to feel about that. 'But maybe there will be a new drug? In the future?'

'Maybe,' Mum said.

'So how would we pay for it?' I asked. 'Would the bank give us the money?'

'Oh, Miranda, for goodness'—'

Gran cut across her. 'I think what your mother means, Miranda, is that we don't need to worry about that now. The main thing is that Gemma is making good progress at the moment.'

'Is that what you mean, Mum?' I asked.

'That's right,' Mum said. 'That's it. More or less.'

CHAPTER TWENTY
No Miracles

I was feeling quite depressed after all that, even though Gemma is doing quite well.

When I went to bed, I told Lucy Fur that I thought maybe I can't make miracles after all, and maybe there are no miracles anyway, and she said, *Oh, I wouldn't go as far as to say that, Miranda. The sun comes up every morning.*

'That's just nature,' I said. 'Astronomy. Look, let's face it, Lucy Fur, I can't write miracles.'

I wouldn't go that far, Lucy Fur said again. *There were the chicks, for example.*

As miracles go, though, that is kind of lame, isn't it? No offence to chicks and chick-lovers, but it doesn't come anywhere near a miracle cure for an incurable condition, which is what I have been angling for, obviously.

What were you expecting? asked Lucy Fur, when I didn't say anything.

'A happy ending,' I said. 'Like in stories.'

The thing about life . . . said Lucy Fur. She is a very philosophical bear, in case you haven't noticed. *The thing about life is, you don't get happy endings. But you do get new beginnings. All the time.*

New beginnings sound like hard work to me. In my personal opinion, life sucks.

I told Miss Lucey that in the morning, about how there are no miracles really.

Miss Lucey said, 'I was in Paris last year, Miranda.'

It is astonishing, in my personal opinion, how people keep coming back to the same old stories. Even when they are supposed to be listening to *your* story.

'Yes,' I said. 'You told us.'

'And there is this church there.'

There are millions of churches in Paris, as a matter of fact. And I have been in a good fifty per cent of them, which is what happens when you travel with adults, but I didn't mention that, because she was off on her Paris riff and you can't stop her when she gets like that.

'And in this church, way back in the eighteenth century, there were so many people being cured of their diseases that the king passed an edict forbidding God to work any more miracles there, because it was getting out of hand.'

She laughed and I laughed. Because that is kind of funny all right.

That proves nothing, though.

'Do you remember, Miranda,' she said, 'when you asked me before what a miracle is, and I said—'

'You said, it is when something is impossible but you can imagine it anyway. That's not right, though. It's when something is impossible but you can *believe* it anyway.'

'Well,' said Miss Lucey, 'that might be a better definition. But the important thing is, you have to have the imagination to make miracles happen, Miranda. That is really all you need.'

Like I said, grown-ups talk in riddles.

CHAPTER TWENTY-ONE
Although Maybe ...

Caroline O'Rourke and Darren Hoey have got quite
pally lately. COR always used to be mean about him. I
think maybe it was that time when they both won Word
of the Day. They started to like each other a bit better.
Or possibly it was the Milky Bar. So that is kind of
miraculous, I have to say.

So anyway, the pair of them came up to me in the
schoolyard at little break and they said they would like
to talk to me, and I said, 'You *are* talking to me,' and
they said, 'We want to talk properly,' and I said, 'We are
talking properly. At least, I am talking properly.' Well,
you know, I'd had a bad week.

So then they looked at each other and they looked at
me and they looked back at each other.

'Well?' I said. 'What is it? Have you two got engaged

or something?'

'No,' said Darren.

'NOOOOOOOOOOOO!' screeched COR.

'Well, then? Are you on the same soccer team maybe?'

'We've been on the same soccer team for three months,' said COR. 'But, listen, it's not about soccer, it's about the money.'

'What money are you talking about, exactly?' I said. I knew the answer, really, but I just wanted to be sure we were all talking about the same thing.

'The two hundred and seventy-three euro and nineteen cents,' said COR. 'The money we raised by mistake, for your gran.'

There was something wrong with that sentence, but I let it go.

'Not my problem,' I said quickly.

'No, we know it's not,' COR said. 'But we can't give it back to the people. We don't know who gave it, we don't know how much anyone gave. People could be coming and saying, "I gave a hundred euro," and it might not be true.'

You can bet it wouldn't be true.

'Not my problem,' I said again.

'So we thought we could give it to a charity of your choice,' COR finished. 'That was Miss Lucey's idea, actually.'

'*My* choice? What's it got to do with me?'

'To say sorry for . . . um . . . embarrassing you like that,' Darren said.

That was the first thing he'd said in this conversation apart from 'No'.

I looked at him.

'*You* didn't embarrass me, Darren,' I said. 'Actually, you were . . . um . . . well, actually, thank you. For, you know, stopping me from, you know . . .'

'Falling over,' he added helpfully.

Oh, Darren!

'Yeah, it was all my fault and I'm sorry,' COR said, 'so have you got a favourite charity?'

Well of course I have a favourite charity. I have a favourite sister who is sick, and they are always looking for money for the hospital and the research and everything. But I didn't want to go into all that just at that moment.

I will, though. I'll tell COR all about it. I think that would be a good plan. She is a good friend and what is the point of having a good friend if you don't tell her about the things that are worrying you?

But for the moment, I just tapped the side of my nose and said I would think about it.

Darren gave me a big smile.

He's OK really.

CHAPTER TWENTY-TWO
The Wishing Well Miracle

Apparently Gemma has been asking for me. I mean, asking to see me. Dad rang to see if I would be able to visit her. He is still in Dublin, obviously.

'But they don't allow children,' I wailed. Though actually they do, sometimes. I have been there before.

'They've made an exception,' Dad said. 'As long as you gown up and don't stay too long.'

Gowning up means putting on these stupid plastic aprons and gloves and putting your hair in a kind of cap thing. It would be much better if it was more like a space suit. Also much cooler. (Although also hotter.)

It sounded to me as if Gemma was going to die after all if they were bending the rules to let me in to see her. But Dad said the doctor thought it would do her good.

Do. Her. *Good*.

To see – *me*!

I must make the acquaintance of this excellent doctor.

So I said, yes please, I would love to visit Gemma. Obviously.

I am making her a special present and it is going to be a story about the wishing well.

I have found that it's much harder writing a story than those little scraps of things Miss Lucey gets us to do for school. *Much* harder. That is the exact opposite of what adults mostly say. They say writing stories is 'lovely', 'great fun', 'so creative' and blah, blah, they'd wear you out the way they go on about it. They need their heads examined. Writing a few paragraphs about something you did at school and already know all about is dead easy. (Unless you are Darren Hoey, I suppose.)

I really, really, really hope she loves it.

Gemma was sitting beside her bed. That was good. Sometimes she is lying in bed because she has no energy, but sitting up is good.

'Hello, Miranda,' she said and she smiled at me. 'Good to see you.'

'I am very sorry about Josh,' I blurted out. I hadn't planned to say that, I didn't want to be reminding her.

(But she could hardly forget, could she?)

Her eyes misted over for a moment but then she blinked and smiled again.

'Dad says you have brought me a very special present. Is it something to eat?'

One-track mind, that girl.

'No,' I said.

'To wear?' she asked.

'No,' I said. 'To read.'

'Oh,' she said. 'I never read *Treasure Island*, I have to admit.'

'This is different,' I said. 'It's not a book. It's a miracle.'

'What?'

Well, there was no point in explaining, so I just said, 'I wrote it for you.' Then I had a brilliant idea. 'Would you like me to read it to you?'

'Eh . . .' she said. 'I would, yes. Nobody has ever read me a – miracle before.'

So I read it to her:

The Wishing Well
A Miraculous Tale
By Miranda Maguire

Prelude

You have to imagine this island and you have to call it Magnanimous, because that is a magnificent word and it is a most splendid and magnificent place. (Because I invented it.)

At the centre of Magnanimous is a fabulous city with silver gates, and it is called Splendiferous, because it is.

Not far from the city of Splendiferous, on the side of an Airy Mountain, there stands the Crystal-clear Glass Hospital for Getting-better Children, and in the hospital, swinging gently back and forth on her royal blue hammock, languishes the Fairy Princess Gem. What she is doing in the Crystal-clear Glass Hospital is trying to get better, because that is what the hospital is for, but she is not really well and maybe she never will be.

It is also a hospital for animals, by the way. But not for grown-ups. Because of all the glass and no curtains. Grown-ups like curtains on the windows.

From time to time, the staff come by with little glass plates of liquorice allsorts and leave them dotted about the room. This is a mistake. They are intended as decorations, because they are so pretty, but everyone thinks they are for eating, so they do.

First movement: Allegretto

It is rumoured abroad that a maiden has made landfall on the beauteous isle of Magnanimous, and indeed it is true. The maiden in question, the Lady Anastasia (well, it's out now anyway), docked some time after dawn and moored her vessel before setting out to find the Crystal-clear Glass Hospital.

As she made her way across the island, the Lady Anastasia helped herself to the fruit of the breadfruit trees that lined her path. As a matter of fact, there were all different kinds of breadfruit trees. Some had little triangular ham sandwiches hanging from them, some had buttered slices of barmbrack, one even had scones with jam.

As she sauntered along, listening to the delightful birdsong and munching on an almond croissant, Anastasia's ears were assaulted by a dreadful screeching. She could not tell who was doing it, but then the most amazing peacock came strutting out of this jungly looking forest (that would be Where the Apes Are, she thought to herself, remembering a map she had seen of Magnanimous, and maybe the monkeys with lollipop paws). The peacock stood right in front of her and casually fanned out his most enormous and spectacular tail  of blue and green and gold and vermilion feathers, all eyes. It was pretty clear that he did not want the Lady Anastasia to enter the forest.

But she didn't want to go into the forest anyway. She was headed for the Airy Mountain and the Crystal-clear Glass Hospital.

So she ignored the peacock and continued walking along by the edge of the forest, which smelt heavenly, all pine and mosses and sweet violets, and the air shivered with sunshine that came glimmering and sparkling through the dark shadows of the branches and it was lovely. She was walking and skipping and singing to herself for what felt like about a day and a half but was probably more like forty minutes, when she came upon a giraffe with her hooves stuck in four buckets. She was wearing a policeman's helmet, like Mr Plod, and when she lowered her head to examine the Lady Anastasia, the helmet did not fall off.

(Anastasia had no idea how that worked. Hat elastic maybe?)

'Are your feet killing you in those shoes?' Anastasia asked the police-giraffe, and the giraffe nodded her helmet and gave a low, snuffly, double-bass kind of sound.

The buckets were a good clue, thought Anastasia. Footrot treatment for sure. So this was one sick giraffe.

'Are you on your way to the hospital, by any chance?' she asked, and the helmet gave a nod again. Clearly, the giraffes around there spoke Metronome as well as Double Bass.

Next thing, the giraffe lowered herself down onto the ground, as if she was a Lego version of the Eiffel Tower only with hinges, and folded her legs in under her. She nodded the Plod helmet again, so the Lady Anastasia got the message. She climbed up on the giraffe's back, and the giraffe stood up again. That was kind of like being on a reverse roller coaster, but she hung on, and then off they went, clunkety-clank, the giraffe taking big awkward noisy steps with her bucketed feet, as if she were trying to avoid trampling on chicks.

After another day and a half of travelling, or in other words forty minutes, the Lady Anastasia arrived at the Crystal-clear Glass Hospital and, taking leave of her mount, she went in search of the Fairy Princess Gem.

The Fairy Princess Gem was busy swinging away gently on her royal blue hammock and fanning herself decorously with her peacock-feather fan, and when she saw the Lady Anastasia approaching she said, 'Did you get it?'

This question perplexed the Lady Anastasia, for she had no idea what it was she was supposed to have got.

So the Fairy Princess Gem explained that she needed a special kind of medicine to make her properly better, and the Lady Anastasia said eagerly, 'I will get it for you, dear sister, as long as it does not cost a million doubloons, for alas I haven't two doubloons to rub together at all. Nor even one.'

'Doubloons are not necessary,' sang the Fairy Princess Gem in Imelda May, a language that the Lady Anastasia found she had no difficulty in understanding, for her own mother was fluent in it.

'What I need is a half a coconut shell of Crystal-clear Water from the Wondrous Wishing Well. That will make me feel better.'

The Fairy Princess Gem explained that not far from the Crystal-clear Glass Hospital for Getting-better Children there is a Deep Dark Forest. That'd be Where the Apes Are, thought the Lady Anastasia. And the peacock.

'But even though it is a Deep Dark Forest,' the Fairy Princess Gem continued, 'there are many clearings there, where the sun comes streaming in, and in one of these clearings, known locally as the Melodious Glade, is a Wondrous Wishing Well, all decked about with fragrant flowers and bejewelled peacocks. The air is sweetly scented and all day long the blackbirds sing Mellifluous in the trees. (That is not a mistake. It's a language. A dialect of Music, if you want to know.) It is all verdant and vermilion, as a matter of fact. And if you lower the water pail into the Wondrous Wishing Well and you draw up the Crystal-clear Water, you can make a wish as you do so and then if you give the Crystal-clear Water to one you truly love to drink, the wish will come true. Or as true as it can come.'

'A miracle,' whispered the Lady Anastasia in wonderment.

'Well, close enough,' said the Fairy Princess Gem and drifted off to sleep.

Second movement: Presto

So the Lady Anastasia took her leave of the Fairy Princess Gem fast and she dashed out in search of the Wondrous Wishing Well.

The bucket-footed giraffe, who was still outside the hospital, offered to take her where she wanted to go, but the Lady Anastasia's bottom was, in truth, a little sore from the first ride she'd taken on giraffe-back, and besides she was pretty sure she could make it to the Melodious Glade much quicker under her own steam, so she declined gracefully, as only a Lady named Anastasia can, and sprinted off in the direction indicated by the kindly giraffe.

Without the encumbrance of foot-buckets, the Lady Anastasia came speedily to the Wondrous Wishing Well, which was as described by the Fairy Princess Gem.

Third movement: Furioso

There were all kinds of amazing things lying around the well and hanging on nearby trees. Jewels and ball-gowns and birthday cakes and sports cars and iPads and squishy armchairs and wedding dresses and water-skis. It was like a very posh department store, only out of doors and higgledy-piggledy.

The Lady Anastasia was not one bit impressed by this random jumble lying about in the Melodious Glade. She was viewing it all with a disdainful frown when a parrot landed on her shoulder with a clunk and a loud squawk of protest, as if someone had pushed him out of the branches of a weeping willow that was weeping copiously into the Wondrous Wishing Well.

'Exterminate the filthy fowl,' the parrot cackled right into the Lady Anastasia's ear. 'It's your only option if you want to approach the Wishing Well.'

Anastasia's head was ringing with the noise the parrot was making, but she did her best to be polite.

'Your English is excellent,' she offered.

'Of course it is,' snorted the parrot and dug his claws into Anastasia's shoulder. It hurt. 'That's because I'm a parrot. That's what we do. Learn languages.'

'Oh,' said Anastasia 'I suppose . . .'

'I advise you to suppose nothing.' The parrot was cackling on. 'Nothing.'

'Well then,' said the Lady Anastasia, 'perhaps you can explain to me what all these things are doing here.' She gestured towards the iPads and sofas and stuff.

'Those are the things the foolish wished for,' rasped the parrot crankily. 'Be careful what you wish for.'

Well, thought Anastasia, she certainly wasn't going to wish for stupid stuff like this. She was going to wish for the Fairy Princess Gem to be well. That was simple enough.

'Do not be taken in by their showy outfits,' the parrot was saying now.

Anastasia looked around but could see nobody in showy outfits. This parrot was really starting to annoy her.

'Filthy creatures,' the parrot squawked on. 'And they . . . er . . . muddy the waters, you know, something dreadful. It shouldn't be allowed. In a better regulated country, it wouldn't happen.'

Ignoring the cranky creature, Anastasia looked about for the water pail to draw the Crystal-clear Water from the Wishing Well, but as soon as she put her hand to it, three howling, screeching, flapping creatures came swooping out of the trees surrounding the Melodious Glade and landed raucously on the ground between the Lady Anastasia and the Wishing Well.

It was three enormous peacocks. They went strutting and striding and preening up and down, up and down, and then they all turned like a troupe of dancers and spread their luminous fantails, forming an effective screen for the well. There was no way the Lady Anastasia was going to be able to get anywhere near it.

'Shoot them!' screeched the parrot. 'It's the only way.' And with that, it flashed off in a swoosh of red and blue and yellow, like an upward streak of lightning, and disappeared back into the weeping willow.

The Lady Anastasia did not approve of blood-sports, but she was desperate to get to the Wishing Well, so she looked around for a gun. There was no gun, but there at her feet was a heap of lustrous pearls, all milky blues and creamy violets and soft pinks, and lying on top of the glimmering mound was a catapult. The Lady Anastasia had never used one of these, but she'd seen pictures, so she picked it up, loaded it with pearlshot, took aim and shot the three peacocks, bim-bam-bim, and they all fell right over. Probably not dead. Just stunned. But anyway lying down, not standing up.

So the Lady Anastasia leapt nimbly over their prostrate bodies and lowered the pail swiftly into the Wishing Well. She squeezed her eyes tight shut and wished hard as she drew up a bucketful of crystal-clear Water and scurried off back to the Crystal-clear Glass Hospital with the precious magic medicine.

Fourth movement: Andante cantabile

The Lady Anastasia arrived at the hammock-side of the Fairy Princess Gem with her pail of water. The Fairy Princess Gem gave her a wonderful smile and handed her half a coconut shell to scoop out the water.

'Did you draw the Crystal-clear Water from the Wondrous Wishing Well?' she asked, as she sipped.

'Yes,' whispered the Lady Anastasia.

'And did you wish?' asked the Fairy Princess Gem.

'Yes,' whispered the Lady Anastasia.

'And did you give it to someone you truly love?' asked the Fairy Princess Gem, still sipping delightedly.

'Yes,' whispered the Lady Anastasia. 'Yes, yes, yes.'

'Well then,' said the Fairy Princess Gem. 'Then there will be a miracle.'

'How are you feeling?' asked the Lady Anastasia.

'Wonderful,' said the Fairy Princess Gem, and she slid out of her hammock and did a little pirouette around her sister to show how wonderful she felt.

So then the Lady Anastasia took the Fairy Princess Gem's hands and they did a stately little dance together, all around the Crystal-clear Glass Hospital, and all the creatures in it called out and whistled and chirped and sang and wuffled and snorted and cried: 'A miracle, a miracle! The Lady Anstasia has wrought a miracle, and the Fairy Princess Gem is well well, well. Hurray!'

Finale

I stopped reading because I had come to the end of the story.

'What do you think?' I asked.

Gemma stood up and she took my two hands and she said, 'Let's dance!'

'Are you feeling better?' I asked.

'Oh, much better,' she said. 'You have no idea how much better.'

And we waltzed around her bed and then we waltzed out of the door (though she is not supposed to leave her room) and we waltzed all the way to the nurses' station, Gemma in her pyjamas and me with my face mask hanging around my neck (because you can't read a story with a face mask on, I mean, come *on*!), and the ward

sister looked up at us and she laughed and said, 'Well, young lady, you are a lot better, I see,' and Gemma laughed too but she said nothing and we waltzed back to her room and back around her bed and eventually she sat down again and I sat opposite her and she said, 'You're right. It's miraculous, Miranda!'

'Yeah,' I said. 'That's me, Miraculous Miranda.'

Describe miracle	Who made it happen	Observations
The people who went to sea in a sieve, they did, in a sieve they went to sea – and they weren't drowned.	Edward Lear, old-timer poet	It only happened in a poem so it is not really real.
Miracles of Modern Medicine	Scientists, surgeons, pharmacologists	Sometimes they work, sometimes they don't.
Cures at Lourdes	Holy Mary	Ditto
Gran gave up the cigarettes.	I wrote about it in one of my essays.	She went back on them, though. Not a miracle.
Lucy Fur can talk.	I just made that up.	But it is a secret.
Darren Hoey turns out to have a mellifluous voice.	This happened all by itself.	The world is a miraculous kind of place.
Darren was nice to me when I nearly fainted in the concert when COR told everyone my secret middle name.	I did say I was going to do a Darren Project to make Darren nice.	To be honest, I only really thought it up, I didn't actually write it in an essay or anything, so I may not have personally caused this miracle.
Chicks arrived out of nowhere.	Possibility (a) The Tooth Fairy brought them. Possibility (b) Gran secretly got them for me. Possibility (c) I wrote about them in an essay and that made the miracle.	Possibility (c) is my favourite explanation.
Ice knives for operations, which don't hurt	I wrote about this in Fantasy Geography and then it turns out that there really are lasers in the world. Gran told me about them.	I am not sure if this is a miracle or not, but it is a very good thing anyway.

Cloud pink eggs from black-and-white speckled chickens	Hasn't happened yet.	Fingers crossed.
Gemma's infection gets cured.	I tried to fix this in Fantasy Geography by sending the giraffes to the bacteria farm.	Hm, well.
Darren gave me a Milky Bar.	Guilt or the Darren Project	I am hoping that Darren is starting to learn to be nice because he sees how lovely me and COR are, but I can't be sure.
Thousands of people were being cured of their diseases in a church in Paris in the 18th century.	According to Miss Lucey.	The king didn't like it and he forbade God to do any more miracles. This was probably a mistake. We all need miracles.
Darren and COR have got pally.	I don't know who made that happen.	It is a mystery.
Gemma's operation is a success and we do a dance to celebrate.	I wrote this in my miracle story.	It might not be a miracle, technically. But it's good.

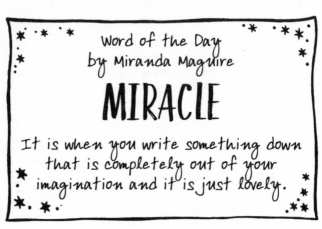

Word of the Day
by Miranda Maguire

MIRACLE

It is when you write something down that is completely out of your imagination and it is just lovely.

THE END

Acknowledgements

I am very grateful to the Centre culturel irlandais in Paris, where I had a residency when I was working on this novel.

Thanks to the Ní Ríordáin O'Mahony family in Paris for their unflagging support and inspiration.

Thanks also to Paula Leyden, Valerie Coghlan, Gráinne Clear, my husband Roger Bennett and my son Matthew Parkinson-Bennett for reading drafts of the text.

I am very grateful to my perceptive, creative and hugely supportive publisher, Anne McNeil of Hodder Children's Books, and to her talented editorial team; also to my agent Sophie Hicks, who is unfailingly enthusiastic and helpful.

Thank you to Orla Tinsley for the inspiration.

And, if he can hear me, thanks also to Edward Lear for being Edward Lear.